CONTENTS

REUBEN HAYES

ALL THINGS WESTERN

By S. Cox

ThunderTree
Keeper Tyree
Sheriff Tyree

By Sandra Cox

Westerns with Romantic Elements

Gwen Slade, Bounty Hunter
TumbleStar
Silverhills
Return to Silverhills

Time Travel Western Romance

Geller's Find
Montana Shootists
Sundial

Modern Day Shapeshifter Western Romance

Mateo's Law
Mateo's Blood Brother

Mateo's Woman

AND MORE

Romantic Suspense with a touch of Paranormal
The Crystal
Paranormal Romance
Tall, Dark and Undead

Romantic Suspense
Queen of Diamonds

Young Adult Series
Mutants
Love, Lattes, and Mutants
Love, Lattes, and Danger
Love, Lattes, and Angel

Young Adult
Minder
Ghost For Sale

Anthologies
Parallels: Felix Was Here

Backlist
Shardai
Akasha

Makita
Odin Cats
Miss Redmond's Deception
Boji Stones
Flower Gardens and More
Rose Quartz
Black Opal

Retired
Vampire Island
Moon Watchers
Vampire Bay
Power Stones
Sunset

ALL RIGHTS RESERVED

A TIP OF THE HAT TO

Beta Readers
Shane Blanchard
Mike Cox
D. L. Finn
Chris Yockey

Copy Editor
Chris Yockey

Research Assistant
Shane Blanchard

Ideas Slingers
Mike Cox
D. L. Finn

ARC-ers
Jacqui Murray
Joe Congel
D. K. Deters

IT Guru

Sonya Blanchard

DEDICATED TO

You, the reader

CHARACTER INDEX

Main Characters
Reuben Hayes, Rancher
Soggy, Horace Eugene Winthrop, Cook and Housekeeper
Katherine Walsh Baylor, Mother of Sage
Sage Baylor, Daughter of Katherine
Hawk, Gunslinger
James Baylor, Senator, Sage's dad. Katherine's husband.

Cowboys
Henry
Billy
Levi, Foreman
Jose Cabrera
Abe Ellis

Townsfolk
Mz. Agatha Krause, Runs boarding house
Mr. McNeely, Owns mercantile store
John, Marshal of Mobeetie
Joe, Bartender

Misc.
Horace Jackson, Justice Death, Judge

Montana Brown, Hired gun

Jinks Dekker, Works at the telegraph office. The son of the owner.

George Schrijnemakers, aka George Story, Reporter

John Smith aka Jack Santos, Killer

Jimmy Lee Jones, Gunslinger

Wild roan, Ole Blue

Wild mare, Darling

Colt, Thunder

CHAPTER 1

April 1880
Texas

Cattle lowed. Horses whinnied. Men whooped and lariats slapped against chaps.

The sounds carried on a thick, heavy breeze. Dust rose from hundreds of hooves, making breathing difficult. The scent of scorched fur and hide filled the air as brands came down on heaving flanks before struggling longhorns were let go.

Reuben Hayes rose in the stirrups, cupped his hands and shouted, "Henry, get that loco longhorn that's headed for the brush."

A lean cowboy raised a hand in acknowledgement, urged his horse into a gallop and shot off after the steer. Another rider came thundering up. This one young, still in his teens. He reined in his foam-flecked dun mare.

"Soggy wants you back at the house pronto. His words not mine, sir." He pushed back his hat and wiped his sweating brow, unruly black curls falling over his forehead.

"What's wrong?" Reuben's raspy voice came out harsh as tension crawled up his backbone. Soggy would never call him back to the ranch if it weren't dire.

"There's a visitor waiting."

"A visitor?" Thick, dark eyebrows, streaked with gray, rose nearly to his hairline. "Soggy told you to come and get me 'cause he has a visitor?" He lifted his voice to carry over the bellow of frightened cattle.

"Not him, Boss. You."

"Thanks for clarifying that, Billy." Eyebrows that had risen now settled into an aggrieved scowl.

Billy wiped a sweaty hand on his pants and swallowed, his Adam's apple doing a nervous dance. "It's a young lady," he added helpfully.

"A young lady?" Reuben's head jerked back and he blinked in surprise.

"Yes, sir."

"A young lady?" he repeated.

"Yes, sir. Pretty as a picture."

For a moment a fatuous look settled over the young man's features, making him look like a moonling calf, Reuben thought in disgust.

"Guess I'm heading back to the ranch." Curiosity warred with irritation. It was branding time. He didn't need to be shunting back and forth between the house and the range like a damn fool. He blew out an impatient breath, lifted the reins, then bellowed, "Levi."

His foreman, a middle-aged man with weathered features and graying hair put heels to his bay and came galloping toward him.

"Yes, Boss?"

"I'm heading back to the house. You're in charge."

"Everything okay?" His foreman took off his no-frills, worn cowboy hat, wiped his forehead then settled it back on his head.

"The boss has a visitor. Pretty as a picture," Billy interjected.

"Oh, yeah?" Levi grinned and spat a wad of tobacco.

"Wipe that smile off your face and take care of the cattle."

Levi complied though his lips continued to twitch.

Reuben pointed a finger at Billy. "You help him." He clapped heels to his big Appaloosa and galloped off.

Once outside the trampled branding area, more tufts of scruffy grass sprang up in the red caliche soil along with yellow and blue wild flowers. Persistent carroty-colored dust spurted in the air with every thump of his horse's large hooves. The rosy hues of the morning sky reflected on canyon walls, turning them a soft pinkie color, as alluring as a beautiful woman. Texas was harsh and survival wasn't easy, but he loved her passionately. More than he'd loved any woman—with the exception of one.

Forty minutes later, he galloped down a low ridge where his rangy ranch house nestled in the center of a wide canyon that ranged five miles or better across. The sun hit the white poplar that loomed over the east side of the house and turned the leaves silver, flashing a halo of color on the pine-stained planks of the structure. A river rock chimney rose on the opposite side. Impatience warred with chest-swelling pride as he rode into his valley and saw his ranch.

But much as he enjoyed the view, he needed to get back to the roundup.

He swung out of the saddle, tied the Appaloosa to the hitching post in front of the house, and tromped inside.

"Soggy," he hollered as he veered toward the living area then ground to a halt, his boot heels digging into the pine planks of the floor.

His legs froze. His breath caught.

A young woman stood in front of the large, river rock fireplace, gazing up at a painting of the ranch that he'd wheedled Alexandria O'Malley into doing after he'd seen her work displayed around the Silverhills' ranch house. The painter had caught the wild feel of the valley in the middle of a ferocious thunderstorm. The ranch house, the solid in the midst of chaos and danger, as lightning struck to the right of it. But the painting wasn't what held his attention now.

The hair on the back of his neck rose and his fingers pricked. He hadn't seen her in near nineteen years but even with her back to him, he'd recognize her anywhere. She wore a black silk dress that fit her like a glove and looked more stylish than what one normally saw in these parts. She hadn't aged a day.

How was that possible when he looked like a piece of old cowhide, leathery and tough? The woman who haunted him still had the same slender figure and the same wild mane of glossy chestnut hair, now sleek and smoothed at the nape of her neck instead of in disarray around her shoulders. The warm scent of lavender that always enveloped her drifted his way.

He opened his mouth to call her name, but his dry throat lacked spittle. He couldn't do more than croak. He swallowed and tried again. "Katherine?" The word a dry whisper.

She turned.

The eyes. The eyes weren't Katherine's. Instead of blue bonnet bright, they were stormy sea gray. But everything else so close it made his heart hurt.

She approached with a warm familiar smile. Katherine's smile. Her hand held out in front of her. "That was my mom. I'm her daughter Sage."

Over the thundering of his heart and the ringing in his ears, one word registered. "Was?"

Her smile faltered and she dropped her hand. Sadness filled those sharp gray eyes. His throat tightened as if the neck of his shirt had shrunk two sizes. He didn't linger on the eyes. Instead, studied the shape of her face, the high cheekbones, the winged brows, full lips, a stubborn rounded chin, a nose that fit her oval-shaped face, and the russet highlights glinting in her hair. Her bones delicate, but if they were Katherine's they were strong. No not lavender, he thought irrelevantly, she smelled like verbena.

"What happened?" Even to his own ears his gritty voice sounded rougher than normal. His hands clenched and unclenched as he drew air into tight lungs.

"Influenza."

"When?" Again, the gravel in his voice more pronounced.

"Two months ago."

He turned and stared out the wide window on the east wall into the distance, at the red and pink arroyo walls, a blue Texas sky, and stunted pines that an eagle soared over. He wheeled abruptly. Too much sunshine. Too much bright. He would have preferred the stormy weather caught in the painting, harsh and out of control like his feelings.

He cleared his throat. "Your father's the senator?" Why did he ask? He knew that. He'd known Katherine had married. Even knew they'd had a child. But he never expected the proof of that union to be standing in his living area, looking like she belonged.

"That's right."

He rocked on his heels and put his hands deep in his pockets, keeping his face impassive, not allowing his grief to leak through. All the while drinking in her features, Katherine's features. And trying not to stare at eyes that didn't match the rest of Katherine's face.

He swallowed past the lump that kept rising in his throat and finally said, "May I ask what you're doing here?"

Sage dug into a small crocheted black purse with a gold link handle and a small, pink cabbage-rose on the front, and handed him an envelope. He stared at it, turning it over and over in his hand. It had been over eighteen years since he'd seen that handwriting.

"I found it when I was going through her effects after the funeral."

"You could have just mailed it." He scrunched it in his big hand and brought it firmly to his side so she wouldn't see the trembles. Reuben Hayes didn't stumble nor shake and this young woman had reduced him to both.

"I was curious. Why would my mother write a letter on her death bed—at least I'm assuming that's when she wrote it—to a man I'd never heard of? Knew nothing about." She looked him over. Her expression frank, inquisitive and just a little disbelieving.

He nearly snorted seeing himself reflected in those gray eyes. A big bulky man, butt-ugly with a nose twice broken and a scar under his right eye, wearing a worn red shirt and tan canvas vest and chaps. Well, to be perfectly honest, he'd never known what Katherine had seen in him either. Katherine, with her vivacious manner and smile, who lit up a room just by being in it.

"Are you going to read it?"

"I'll read it later." He shoved it in his vest pocket, proud his hand didn't shake. "Miss Sage—"

Before he could say more, Soggy came hustling in, wiping his hands on a white towel with cinnamon spattered on it, wrapped around his middle. A touch of flour on a bewhiskered cheek.

"Miss Sage, there's cinnamon rolls fresh out of the oven. You come on in the kitchen now." He turned to Reuben. "Boss."

They looked at each other over the young lady's head, Soggy's expression troubled. Soggy had known Katherine too. He and Soggy had been together since

Reuben was a young man trying to start up this ranch. Both had been younger then.

"If it's not an imposition, Mister—"

"Horace Eugene Winthrop. My parents were as poor as dirt, but my momma wanted me to at least have an important sounding name, but you can call me Soggy. Everyone does. Guess I should have introduced myself out on the porch when you told me who you was." Soggy gave her a rare smile.

She smiled back.

"You got your momma's smile." Soggy's bushy white eyebrows went up and his breath hitched.

"You knew my mother?" Her lips parted and her eyes lit up.

"I did."

"I'd love to hear how you knew her."

"You come on in the kitchen and eat your cinnamon roll and I'll tell you all about it."

"I don't want to impose." She hesitated.

"Soggy don't make his famous cinnamon rolls for just anybody. You best take advantage of it." His hands in his pockets, Reuben rocked back on his heels.

"Then what are we waiting for?" She gave a rolling laugh. A laugh filled with joy. One he hadn't heard in years. Again, his breath hitched.

Reuben gestured her forward.

They trooped through a short hallway that opened into a dining area which segued into the kitchen. Plain white curtains fluttered at an open window, while the scent of earth, pine and fresh rolled in, mixing with the overlaying scent of cinnamon that hung in the air.

Sage's curious gaze swept the clean, spartan space. A room devoid of any feminine frills.

"Sit. Sit." Soggy motioned her toward a long, planked pine table, opened the cast-iron wood-burning oven and pulled out a tray that held a couple of dozen cinnamon rolls.

Reuben pulled out a hard-backed wood chair and with a rustle of silk, Sage sank into it.

She sniffed the air. "Those smell wonderful, Mr. Winthrop."

"Soggy."

"Soggy."

He plunked a white mug of rich, steaming coffee in front of her along with a plain white plate that held a large yeasty cinnamon roll. She bit into it, chewed, swallowed then exclaimed, "This is the best cinnamon roll I've ever ate."

"Best you'll find in the state of Texas." The little man preened. "Though Cookie's are a close second," he added grudgingly.

"Cookie?"

"The mess cook over at Silverhills."

"They beat anything in Philadelphia too."

If possible, his chest puffed even more, giving him the look of a strutting bantam rooster.

"So, tell me about your mother," Reuben interrupted. Once again, gruffer than his whiskey-laden, cigar-smoking, raspy voice normally sounded.

She carefully set the roll, that she'd just brought to her lips, back down then wiped her fingers and looked him straight in the eye. "Tell me why she wrote to you." She notched her chin in the direction of the letter and straightened her shoulders.

His eyes narrowed, his brows beetled and his gaze bore into her, his lips thin, his features unyielding.

Soggy poured them both more coffee, his lips twitching.

"Something funny?" Reuben turned his intimidating gaze to his cook. But there was no intimidating Soggy. The man had been with him since Reuben was barely out of his teens, and less than ten years his senior, could get away with what no other man could.

"Well, yeah, as a matter of fact. You two look like two mules after the same patch of grass and neither willing to give an inch or go to another patch."

"You're calling me a mule?" Sage's eyes widened. She fairly quivered with affront. Her chin notched up another inch.

"Now don't take that tone with me, missy. Ain't going to do you a bit of good. You may be considered the senator's daughter out east. Here you're just Katherine's child." His voice softened on the last words and his eyes shone suspiciously bright. He dabbed at them with the corner of the towel tied around his narrow waist.

Reuben looked on in astonishment. Soggy was as tough as his hardtack.

Sage's chair scraped against the floor as she jumped out of it and hugged the older man. "I'm so sorry. Of course, you're right. It's none of my business. None at all."

"Humph." Soggy blinked rapidly several times, patted her awkwardly on the shoulder then stepped back. "It's alright, girl. Perfectly normal to wonder what your parent got up to when she was your age."

She returned to her seat and sank into it and once again fixed her attention on Reuben. "Will you tell me about her?"

The muscles in his face and shoulders sagged. When the attitude disappeared, he was pretty sure there was nothing she could ask for that he wouldn't find a way to give her.

He opened his mouth then cleared his throat. No words came.

Soggy jumped in. "Did your momma tell you that she grew up in these parts?"

Sage shook her head. "My momma's childhood was a mystery. She never talked about it."

"She lived on a little ranch located about ten miles from here. At least it used to be, it's nothing but a patch of dirt with a falling down cabin on it now. In fact, Reuben bought the land off ole man Walsh when he decided to pack it in. He took off and no one has heard from him since."

"What about my grandmother?" She leaned forward, her gaze intense.

"She died long before Miss Katherine went East."

"Um." She turned that clear-eyed gaze on Reuben. "And my momma?"

He cleared his throat and his thoughts turned inward. He could see her as if it were yesterday. Could see himself as well. "Your mom always had a hankering to go East. Why I don't know. She was as beautiful and as wild as the West Wind. How could she survive the confines of a city?" He spread his hands and shrugged in bewilderment.

"That explains the frequent trips to the country. She always said she felt stifled. Please go on."

"That last summer two of her cousins from back east came to visit. They brought a friend, your father. When they left, she left with them. Now if you'll excuse me." The chair scraped across the floor as he pushed to his feet and strode out. Soggy on his heels. When he got to the porch and the door slammed behind them, Soggy ground to a stop, his bowlegs splayed, his hands on his hips.

"You let her go, you're a fool twice over."

"Don't go there."

"Or what?" Soggy notched up a thin chin, his expression belligerent.

"I'll fire you."

"You've fired me so many times, I've lost count." The little man snorted.

"I can't do this. Just looking at her is a reminder of Katherine."

"And that's a bad thing?"

"I don't know, Soggy. I just don't know." He took off his hat and ran thick, restless fingers through dark brown hair that had started to thin.

"She's no fool. She's going to look into a mirror one day soon and wonder where those eyes came from, especially now that she's come face to face with yours."

"I'd have never let her go if I'd thought—" He scrubbed his face with his hand.

There was no question to whom he referred.

"Well, you know now."

"So I do." He straightened his shoulders and started toward the door just as Sage came through it.

"I want to thank you for your hospitality and information about my mother." She held out her hand.

He took it, his big callused paw swallowing her dainty fined-boned one and felt a fierce sense of protectiveness wash over him. Something he'd never felt before. When she tugged, he released it reluctantly.

"Where you staying? Mz. Krause's?" The only boarding house in Mobeetie.

"Yes. Until the next stage comes through. Could I hitch a ride into town?"

"Of course. But why not stay here instead? Besides cinnamon rolls, Soggy also makes a mean blackberry cobbler."

"I don't want to impose." But there was no real conviction in her voice.

"No imposition. Maybe it's time to get to know your roots."

Gray eyes looked into gray eyes. "Maybe it is."

CHAPTER 2

Relief washed through him. Surprising in its intensity.

"Good, good. How'd you get here? Old man Harrington?"

"Yes. How did you know?"

The townsfolk send anyone that needs a buggy ride his way. Gives him a little pocket change." He rubbed his hands together. "Well, I'll hitch up the wagon, pick up your luggage and settle your bill." His raspy voice hearty.

"I'll go with you. And thank you, but I'll settle my own bill."

"Now, missy, I can't let you do that. You're my," he paused, then settled on "guest." Rocking on his heels, he shoved his hands into his pocket.

"Can't let me go with you or pay my bill?" She arched an eyebrow that reminded him of a raven's wing.

"Pay the bill."

"I thank you for the offer but I'll pay my own bill."

"I can't let you do that but I'd be mighty happy for the company."

"Mr. Hayes—"

"Reuben."

"Reuben. While I appreciate your gesture of hospitality, I can't let a stranger pay for my account at the boarding house."

"I was a good friend of your mother's. I think that negates us being strangers."

"Still, I pay my own way."

"Lore, you're as stubborn as your mother." Another thought struck him, "Does your," again he paused and cleared his throat, "father know you came all this way alone?"

Her chin notched up. "I'm eighteen. I don't answer to anyone."

"Some might call it common courtesy." He gave her look for look.

She dropped her eyes first, and though her chin still jutted at a determined angle remained silent.

His brows beetled. He'd fought Indians, hung horse thieves and shot rustlers, but he had a feeling that was going to be child's play compared to going up against the determined young woman standing in front of him.

He decided to let the subject drop for the moment.

"I'll get the wagon. Wait here."

Reuben hitched a large-boned bay to the big-wheeled buckboard and drove it the short distance to the house, where Sage sat rocking on one of the two white-painted, old rockers on the porch. The curved bands at the bottom of the chair making a smooth, lulling sound as they moved against the wooden planks of the floor. Her gaze, bright and inquisitive, taking in everything.

In the evening, he could usually be found there himself, a whiskey in hand watching the sunset turn the sky the purdiest shades of red and purple ever seen. Darkening the trees and cattle, in the distance, to a deep ebony. Sometimes Soggy joined him, sometimes not.

Seeing him, she stood and moved toward him, her gait as smooth as that of a young saddle horse. The empty rocker still gently creaking.

The wagon groaned as he jumped down and helped her up, then climbed back on, clucked to the horse and snapped the reins. Sage grabbed the side of the buckboard as the bay took off at a brisk trot. Then catching the rhythm, let go and gazed around her, soaking in everything, much as she had on the porch.

Blinding sunshine warmed his shoulders as they drove under the HAYES RANCH sign, creaking back and forth in the gusts of wind. To the sign's right, an old pine swayed in the breeze. The wind carrying its earthy, resinous scent, washing over them.

She turned toward him, straightening her shoulders.

When talk was not forthcoming, he asked, "Something on your mind?"

She took a deep breath and plunged in, "You were right earlier, about Dad not knowing where I was going. He's so busy he probably won't even realize I'm gone. He's working on a bill to aid and protect Americans' voting rights regardless of background and color. He's traveling around the state. Still, that is no excuse. I'm not a coward. I will send a telegraph when we reach town." She straightened her spine and lifted her chin.

Apparently, admitting she was wrong didn't come any easier to her than it did to him, but all he said was, "You sound even more like your mother. She tempered her independence with kindness and a thought for others." With a short jab of his chin, he gave her a nod of approval then pointed at a large jackrabbit that hopped out from gray-green sagebrush. The bright sun glistening on sleek brown fur.

It gave them an appraising look then flopped lengthy ears and, with a leap through scruffy green grass and spindly brush, disappeared into a handful of shrub pine at the base of the canyon's red and pink craggy walls.

"That was the biggest rabbit I've ever seen." Sage's eyes widened.

"It's a muley."

"A muley?"

"It's what we call jackrabbits around here."

He continued to point out Mother Nature's wonders. A herd of bison in the distance. A doe and her fawn still young enough to have spots. A feral hog with a bushy-tipped tail that had her eyes widening as she leaned over the side for a better look as it quickly trotted out of sight.

He studied his surroundings through the lens of the young woman whose existence he'd known nothing about till a short while ago. She was like a sponge, drawing in all the wonders of this big, beautiful country. Just as he drew in the joy of being with her.

The trip passed much too quickly to his way of thinking. Before he knew it, the bay was trotting into Mobeetie, its big hooves kicking up spurts of dust on the hard-packed ground.

They passed several saloons. Two three-story hotels on opposite ends of the street. And a livery stable with wide double doors, where the clanging of an anvil rang out.

He halted the wagon in front of a neat, white painted one-story building with a large green sign that read MERCANTILE. A barbershop on one side and a gunsmith shop on the other.

"The boarding house is that way." Sage pointed at a side street.

"I know. Thought you might like to take a look in the Mercantile while I run a couple of errands. We can stop by Mz. Krause's on the way out of town."

"That works for me." Skirts rustling, she climbed down from the wagon before he'd brought it to a complete stop. He shook his head. He'd never met a female yet who didn't light up at the chance to shop. Sorta like a man hunting. But they were on the scent of entirely different critters. Muslins and ribbons and teas. Ah well. Females were certainly fascinating creatures.

He tied the horse then stepped on the sidewalk to follow her inside. "Ladies," he swept off his hat as two middle-aged women came bustling by. One plump. One on the thin side.

"Reuben."

"Mr. Hayes."

Both women smiled.

The door bell jangled overhead as he strode into the Mercantile.

"Mr. McNeely." He nodded to a dapper little man behind the counter wearing a white starched shirt, pin-striped trousers and bright red suspenders.

"Reuben. Good to see you. What can I do for you?" Smiling, Mr. McNeely stepped out from behind the counter and gave Reuben's hand a firm shake.

"A friend of mine is visiting from out East. I figured she'd enjoy seeing your fine establishment." He motioned to Sage and she stepped forward and held out her hand.

"Mr. McNeely."

"Miss—"

"Baylor. Sage Baylor."

The store owner gave her a warm smile and shook her hand. "Any friend of Reuben's is a friend of mine. You got people around here?"

"My mother used to live here."

"Baylor. Don't rightly know any Baylors. Do you, Reuben?" He scratched his head.

"My mother not my father. My mother's maiden name was Walsh."

"Walsh. Nope. Don't know any Walshes either. Though, I've only been here about three years."

"They were gone before that." She looked around. "You've got a nice store here. Do you mind if I look at your fabric?" She pointed at the bolts on the far wall.

"Be my guest." The businessman kicked in. "Just got those bolts of silk from St. Louie. Not that we've got much call for it out here, mind. But the ladies have all been in, oohing, aahing and buying them."

"I'll be sure and take a look at them." She nodded and hustled across the room, her skirts swishing, her heels clicking on the wood floor.

Both men watched her walk away.

"Nice young lady."

"Yeah." Hands in his pockets, Reuben rocked on his heels.

"So how do you know her?"

"You planning on starting a newspaper and writing up a society column?" Reuben demanded.

Then relented. "Knew her mom when she lived around here. Keep an eye on her, will you? I've got some errands to run."

"She's safe as houses in here."

Reuben grunted then strode out of the store, the bell once more jangling overhead. He took the wagon to Mz. Krause's, settled up, then hauled a couple of oversized green carpetbags downstairs and threw them in the back of the wagon.

He turned onto Main Street just as Sage came out of the mercantile. She looked around in bewilderment at the empty space where the wagon had been, then caught sight of him. Waving, she started across the street heading in his direction.

She'd taken no more than two steps when a cowboy came weaving down the sidewalk, shooting off his gun. A rider directly across the street—

a greenhorn from the looks of him—lost control of his startled mount as it reared, pawing the sky, then thundered down the street, racing straight at Sage.

Reuben's breath lodged in his throat. He leaned forward in the seat and slapped the reins against the bay's rump.

Traces jangling, the horse leaped forward. Fear coated Reuben's system and beads of icy sweat slicked his forehead. He slapped the reins again, his muscles tensing as he readied himself to jump from the wagon when he drew alongside Sage.

Before he could vault from the seat, a man leapt over the empty hitching post in front of the store, dropped on Sage and, in a cloud of dust, rolled them both out of the way. The panicked horse's hooves landing where Sage had been moments before. The horse thundered on down the street, the greenhorn on his back flopping from side to side in the saddle, his bowler flying off his head.

Sage was covered head to toe by a tall form in a black duster. The only thing visible an errant russet curl splayed against the black canvas covered arm.

"Get off her." He tossed her rescuer aside and yanked Sage to her feet.

"Are you alright?" He ran his callused, thick fingers over her arms, feeling for protruding bones.

"Yeees. I think so."

Relief tore through him and his thundering heart slowed. He straightened the clever little hat, with a perky blue feather, sitting cockeyed on her head then turned his attention to the man rising slowly from the dusty street. Reuben grasped his arm and jerked him the rest of the way up.

"And you, mister. Are you alright?"

"I'm fine. Don't feel the need to pat me down like the young lady there." Pale blue eyes that held an audacious twinkle winked at Reuben.

"I'm Reuben Hayes and I'm in your debt." Reuben held out his hand.

"I'm—"

The stranger started to take Reuben's outstretched paw when Reuben said, his voice cold, his teeth clenched, "Hold that thought."

He'd just caught sight of the cowboy who'd shot off his pistol. Reuben went bulling toward him, his jaw working.

Whiskey fumes hit him from a yard away. He took a long stride forward and fisted his hand in the front of the cowboy's shirt and tightened. "Obadiah, you nearly got my... "guest" killed."

"Now, Reuben, I didn't know—" The man got no farther as a large, hard-knuckled fist connected with his jaw. Obadiah went down without a sound.

Reuben rubbed his scraped knuckles and stepped over him. Fire still burning behind his eyes, he marched to Sage and the stranger who'd saved her.

Sage's eyes were wide. The stranger's gave nothing away. "Hope I don't ever make you mad," he drawled.

"Not likely. You were saying."

"Hawk."

"Got another handle to go with it?"

"Just Hawk."

Reuben looked him up and down, assessing. The light blue eyes looked steadily back. Most people shifted under his gaze, but not this one. Reuben would put him in his early to mid-twenties. Long and lanky. Good-looking, with hair as black as the duster he wore. Hanging open, it revealed a businesslike Colt Navy Revolver. Single action, .36 caliber.

Reuben bent down and picked up a black cowboy hat that had rolled near his feet, hit it against his leg to knock the dust off, and handed it to the young man in front of him.

"Thanks for saving my..." Again, he hesitated. And again ended up with guest. "Not many men would be that quick thinking or acting. That took a lot of guts to do what you did. I owe you."

"You owe me nothing."

"Looking for work? I could always use a good hand at the ranch."

Hawk thrummed his right hand on his thigh considering. "Maybe."

"Maybe?" Reuben's eyebrows shot up.

"I was just getting ready to sit down to a game of cards. If my luck holds and I fill my pockets, I'll be riding on. If it don't, I'll come by the ranch and take you up on that offer. At least temporarily."

"Ma'am." He tipped his hat to Sage then strolled across the street to the Red Horse Saloon.

Sage who'd been unusually quiet, said, "Well, I declare."

Hands in his back pants pockets, he stared at the black duster disappearing through swinging saloon doors. "Yeah."

CHAPTER 3

Early morning air hung heavy and still. A mounted rider hovered at the top of the arroyo, motionless except for a swish of the horse's tail.

The rider's gaze swept the ranch below as the mist dissipated in willowy whisps, leaving in its disappearing trail a blend of color and light. Taking with it the uneasy feel of premonition.

Stained pine planks of the long, rangy house glowed golden in dawn's orangey-pink light. The house nestled in the center of a wide canyon ranging five miles or better across. Silver leaves sparkling, a white poplar shed shade on the east side of the ranch house. The river rock chimney on the opposite end, bereft of rising smoke.

Hawk leaned on his saddle horn. He'd thought long and hard before taking Reuben up on his offer. He had a nest egg he could break into if he decided to move on. But he was intrigued. Reuben Hayes was a legend in Texas. A ranch owner who'd fought off Indians, Comancheros, rustlers, and drought. And won. Reuben might be twenty years Hawk's senior, but he wouldn't want to go up against him. Hayes was fast with a gun and tough as a longhorn bull. Still, he had a reputation for being fair.

What had made him hesitate was his guest. She intrigued him more than Reuben. Normally, he'd follow up on that interest, but being a sane man and not having a death wish, he had no intention of starting up a flirtation with any female under Reuben Hayes' roof. Still and all, some coin jingling in his pocket would be helpful. He'd work a month and move on. Surely, he could stay away from the female and out of trouble that long.

Odd that they both had those steel-colored eyes and non-flinching gaze.

None of his business, he reminded himself and nudged his pinto down the sloping trail to the ranch, causing pebbles to roll under his horse's large hooves.

On level ground, a weathered HAYES RANCH sign swayed and creaked with each gust of wind. His mount ambled along the dirt road till he reached the house. Horses nickered in a nearby corral. Swishing their tails and hanging their heads over the wooden rails. Paint, his pinto, whickered in response. A youth carrying a bale of hay nodded.

He swung out of the saddle and wrapped his reins around the hitching rail, where a saddled Appaloosa stomped on hard-packed earth.

He thumped his knuckles against the door and waited. He didn't have to wait long. An old codger wearing an apron and a belligerent expression stood in the doorway. Laughter escaped from farther in the house. One raw and rusty. One sounded like heaven's bells.

"Yes?" The man had longish gray hair, a close beard and a belligerent expression.

"I'm here to see Mr. Hayes."

"And who might you be?"

"Hawk."

"First or last?"

"Just Hawk. And you are?"

"Horace Eugene Winthrop."

Before the little man could say more, Reuben bellowed, "Soggy, who's at the door?"

"Some bird," Soggy bellowed back.

Momentary silence followed. Then Reuben asked, "Hawk?"

"Yeah, that's it."

"Well, show him in, he saved Sage's life."

The little man's demeanor changed. Welcome replaced belligerence. "Well, why didn't you say so? Come in. Come in." He motioned Hawk to follow. With a bowlegged gait, he strode through the entryway and living room, into a dining area with a long pine table that segued into a small kitchen. A black stove, a kitchen sink with a hand pump and pine cabinets visible. The smell of strong, hot coffee; the fried, floury scent of flapjacks; and the sweet aroma of warm maple syrup melded with laughter that cut off at his entrance, though smiles still remained on Reuben and his guest's features.

"Come on in. Have a seat. Soggy, set another plate." Reuben's chair scraped as he stood and threw down his napkin.

"Thank you."

He picked the chair next to the young lady and held out his hand. "I don't believe we've been properly introduced. "Name is Hawk."

Pleased to meet you, Mr. Hawk. Sage Baylor." She stood and slipped a fine-boned, long-fingered hand into his and gave a firm shake.

"Just Hawk." He blinked, feeling the warmth of her hand all the way down to his toes, along with a rush of blood that held a sizzle of electricity. His ears buzzed.

By the way Miss Baylor's eyes widened, he thought maybe she felt it too.

Reuben cleared his throat.

Hawk and Sage continued to stare at one another.

Reuben cleared his throat again. This time the sound made it through the buzzing. Hawk dropped the young lady's hand like a hot potato.

Soggy, who bustled to the table with a steaming cup of coffee in a plain white mug and a stack of hotcakes, shook his head. "Kids," he muttered under his breath.

"Yeah," Reuben responded then said to Hawk, "Sit down."

Hawk seated Sage, got a grip on himself and dropped into his chair.

Reuben sat down, reached for his coffee and took a gulp. "Mm, that's good coffee, Soggy."

The little man had just pulled out the chair next to Reuben and began to inhale his flapjacks. "Of course, it is," he said after he swallowed.

Reuben turned his attention back to Hawk. "I see you've still got your shirt."

"That's the only thing I didn't lose. That job still available?"

"Certainly."

"I won't be staying much over a month. Is that a problem?"

"Not for you. Depending on how well you work out it may be for me."

"I appreciate it." Hawk shoveled the pancakes in front of him into his mouth, chewed and swallowed. He took another forkful and waved them at Soggy. "These are delicious."

"You won't go hungry while you're here." Soggy shoveled in another mouthful.

"A definite benefit." He threw the older man a grin.

Soggy didn't grin back but at least he wasn't scowling at him.

He shot a casual glance at Reuben then Sage. They looked nothing alike, except for those clear gray eyes that seemed to see right through a man. Where Reuben's were steely, Sage's were reminiscent of the sea, sometimes calm and sometimes stormy.

Both held their chins at a pugnacious angle, willing to take on the world.

They had to be related. Maybe Reuben was her uncle. But if so, why didn't he say so?

"Something on your mind?" Reuben asked, his voice dry, his eyes narrowed.

Hawk threw a quick glance at Sage who watched him curiously and his normal caution shot right out the window.

"I was just wondering—" His intent look returned

to Reuben whose steely gaze arrowed into him and held a warning that anyone but a fool would not ignore. And Hawk's mama—whoever she might be—didn't birth no fool.

"I was just wondering what you'd like me to do." Beads of sweat popped out on his forehead. This was not good. It wasn't like him to be thrown off stride by a pretty face, especially when that pretty face was linked to a cantankerous protector known for having a hasty temper, a fast gun and a hard fist.

"It's branding season. Today's the last day. You can ride out with me." Reuben tossed down his napkin and shoved back his chair.

"Mr. Hayes," Sage said.

"Reuben."

Interesting. Maybe she really was a guest.

"In the excitement yesterday, I forgot to send Dad a telegram." She flashed something between a smile and a grimace.

"We'll need to rectify that."

"Got a horse I can ride?"

"If there's one thing, we've got around here it's horses. If you can wait till tomorrow, I'll take you in."

"I can go by myself."

"No, missy, you can't. You aren't to ride out alone anywhere. And that's not open to argument."

Steely gray met stormy gray. Two chins lifted. Two sets of nostrils flared.

"I can take care of myself."

"Can you shoot?"

"No."

"Once you learn, we'll have this conversation again. Though, it don't mean I'll be changing my mind."

Surprisingly, she backed down.

"Your ranch. Your rules. Can Soggy take me?"

"Sorry, girl, I've got my hands full today. What about young Hawk there?"

Everyone gave the cook a startled look.

"What?" the cook demanded. "He's smart enough to know that if anything goes wrong, you'll string him up, gut him and scalp him. Aren't ya, lad?"

"Yes, sir, I am." Those fine tasting flapjacks turned to lard in his belly. Being anywhere near Sage Baylor was not a good idea and he was pretty sure Reuben knew it. Though, the idea of losing his thick, wavy black hair, that he was justifiably proud of, was enough to cool the blood that had a tendency to heat around the young lady sitting beside him.

"They're just teasing," Sage reassured. "If you don't mind, I really would like to go in town and send that telegram."

He'd been frantically searching for a reason not to take her, but her asking was his undoing. He bit back a sigh and raised an eyebrow at Reuben. "I'd be happy to." Though he was pretty sure his face didn't reflect that.

"I'll have your word that you'll take care of her."

"You have it, sir."

Reuben gave a sharp jerk of his chin. "Let's go pick you out a mount." He looked Sage up and down. "You got riding clothes?"

"I do. Give me a minute and I'll be right back." She threw a blinding smile all around, pushed back her chair before Hawk could reach for it and trotted out of the room.

"Might as well have another cup of coffee." Soggy's chair scraped back as he got up, took a few steps into the kitchen, grabbed a granite pot and came back.

"Yeah, might as well," Reuben echoed, holding up his mug.

In less time than expected, the threesome spilled out of the house and headed for the stables, Sage dressed in a blue split riding skirt and tan shirt.

"Pick your poison." Reuben made a sweeping gesture that encompassed a long row of stalls where horses nickered and snorted as the three of them entered the large, doubled-doored building.

The youth he had seen earlier nodded.

"Billy," Reuben called. "Come over here and meet Sage Baylor and Hawk."

Billy came loping over and drew off one of his leather work gloves.

"It's a pleasure, ma'am. Mr. Hawk."

He shook first Sage's hand then Hawk's.

"Just Hawk," Hawk responded.

"Hawk is going to be working with us for a while."

"Welcome," Billy said.

He looked at Sage and waited expectantly.

Before Sage could respond, Reuben placed rough hands on hips and said, "Better get that hay to the hosses, Billy."

"Yes, sir." He nodded to Sage and Hawk, then loped

back to the bale of hay he'd dropped and headed for the corral.

"Let's find you a hoss." Reuben strode into the barn with the rolling cowboy gait that men who spend a lot of time in the saddle develop.

The comforting scents of hay and horse enveloped them as they strode down the hard-packed earth between stalls, Sage's head swinging from side to side, studying each animal they passed.

A steady thump, thump, thump came from the back of the barn.

"What's that?" Sage craned her head trying to see, her boots kicking up tufts of hay that had dropped from the bale Billy carried.

The thump turned into a thunderous crack.

"Look out," Hawk shouted and leaped, pushing Sage up against a rough-edged stall, protecting her with his body. Reuben dived to the other side as a big blue roan, with black forelegs and head, splintered his stall door, came charging down the aisle, and disappeared through the wide entryway.

Sage shook off Hawk and stepped into the middle of the aisle watching the big stallion kick up dust as it galloped away. A couple of cowboys saw him and took off after him, shouting, but there was no hope of stopping him now.

"That's the horse I want." Hands fisted on hips, she watched the disappearing roan, her eyes sparkling.

"Yeah." Reuben stepped up beside her, his legs splayed, his hands fisted on hips.

The stances eerily similar.

"Though, I wouldn't hold my breath." His voice dry, he clapped his hands together to get the dust off of them. "Are you alright?"

"I'm fine. Mr. Hawk yanked me out of harm's way, again."

"Hawk," Hawk corrected.

"Hawk."

"Looks like I'm even deeper in your debt." Reuben rocked on his heels.

"Not a bit. I haven't done anything that any right-thinking man wouldn't have done," Hawk replied.

"Or woman," Sage threw in.

Hawk grinned and Reuben blinked.

Before anyone could reply, Billy came racing in. "We lost Blue again."

"I can see that, Billy."

"Uh, yeah." Billy ducked his head, an abashed expression on his young features. "Do you want us to go after him?"

"He's long gone. You haven't a hope in hell, in heck," Reuben corrected himself, "of catching him."

"The roan? You've had him before?" Hawk took off his hat then repositioned it on his head.

"Once before. I made the mistake of putting him in the corral. He kicked a section down, took off, taking the mares in the corral with him. That stallion is more gutsy than a lot of men I know."

"Why not just let him run free?" Sage asked.

"Well, he is now, ain't he?" Reuben scowled then said, "Let's find you a hoss to ride then I need to hie out to the branding."

Not much later, Sage mounted on a frisky chestnut mare, whose hide reflected the same reddish highlights as Sage's hair, rode toward Mobeetie beside Hawk. His brown and white pinto trying unsuccessfully to make overtures to the mare. Kicking up dust beneath his hooves, he sidled toward the chestnut.

"Paint, behave yourself." Hawk reined his mount away as his canvas encased leg brushed against Sage's. She shot him a look.

After that he kept a couple of feet between the two mounts.

A jackrabbit darted out of thick underbrush, right under the chestnut's nose. Automatically, Hawk reached for the mare's reins, but Sage had already brought her under control with heels and hands.

"You've got a good seat. A nice way with your horse."

"My momma was horse mad. She taught me to ride almost before I could toddle." She threw him a smile that had him slackening his grip on the reins and Paint sidling back toward the mare.

"Was?"

She died awhile back." The smile slid off her face and her eyes filled with sadness. "That's what brought me out here. I found a letter addressed to Mr. Hayes. Reuben," she corrected herself, "among her possessions. Since she'd never mentioned him, nor had daddy, I was curious. So, I decided to deliver it myself."

"Did you find out what you wanted to know?" One

hand rested casually on his thigh. One held the reins, while the warmth from Paint seeped through the saddle leather beneath him.

She snorted. "You've met Reuben. What do you think?"

"That he's a man of few words."

"Few might be an exaggeration." She grimaced. "All he said was that they grew up together. And when my daddy and my momma's cousins came from out East for a visit, she went back with them."

"And what do you think of Reuben Hayes?"

She didn't hesitate. "That's he got a gruff exterior and a heart of gold."

"He's got a reputation in these parts."

"What kind of reputation?"

"That you don't knowingly go up against him if you want to see the next sunrise."

"And what are your thoughts?"

"That he's tough as old shoe leather but fair."

"Hmm. Seems a fair assessment." She ran a free hand over the chestnut's silky neck then threw a sidewise glance at Hawk. "And you? Do you have a reputation too?"

"Not one that does me much credit." He looked straight ahead.

"So, what did you do to earn this reputation that doesn't do you much credit, besides save women in danger, lose at poker and work as a cowhand?"

"You caught me between jobs."

"And what might those jobs be?"

"You aren't going to let this go, are you?"

"Daddy always said I was curious as a cat."

"How many lives you got left?"

She laughed, a sound that ran through him like a choir of angels singing.

"Pretty sure I've at least five left. So, what do you do?"

He leveled his gaze so that it met hers straight on. "I live by my gun."

CHAPTER 4

Her eyes widened and she jerked the reins, the chestnut tossing its head in protest. A moment later Sage was back in control. "Does Reuben know what you do for a living?"

"He's never said anything, but not much gets past him. That man is shrewd as a fox and ferocious as a wolf."

"Hmm. So, I'm staying with a man who tamed his piece of Texas by force and I'm riding with a gunslinger. Definitely different from my life in St. Louie." She smiled when she said it.

"That pretty much sums it up." The smile softened the words, but they still stung. Why they should was beyond his ken, she spoke the truth. Though he could have done with a little less frankness.

They fell into silence, her brow furrowed in a thoughtful frown as they rode into Mobeetie.

The horses kicked up the well-tamped dirt in the street as they trotted down it. Sturdy buildings made of brick and wood lining each side. Two cowboys galloped by in the opposite direction, one tipping his hat to Sage.

A couple of middle-aged women, one dressed in

sedate brown, one in a pale pink and aqua plaid, hustled down the wide-planked sidewalk, chatting.

A little boy raced around the women after a yellow puppy, nearly knocking down the lady in plaid. He kept going, throwing an apology over his shoulder, and ran straight into a man built like a tree. He stumbled backwards and would have fallen if the man hadn't grabbed him. The gent gave him a few stern words and sent him on his way.

Hawk's lips twitched. Typical boy.

"Any place you need to go besides the telegraph office? The Mercantile perhaps?"

"I need to go to the boarding house and settle my bill."

"I'm guessing Reuben will have taken care of that."

"I told him I would pay it." Her chin notched up.

He didn't say anything, just raised his eyebrows.

"I need to at least check." She sighed.

"Of course."

They pulled in front of a small, wood shingled structure wedged between two large two-story buildings. Gold letters in the front window proclaimed Telegraph Office. Hawk jumped off his horse and putting his hands on Sage's waist, lifted her from the saddle then dropped them immediately, his fingers tingling, much like they did before a gunfight. He flexed them. Once. Twice.

Her breath caught. She took a step back and lifted her chin. "I can dismount on my own."

"Yes, ma'am."

"Sorry. I appreciate the courtesy. I just don't like

anyone thinking I can't take care of myself."

"No chance of that." His lips twitched.

"Well, that's good." She cleared her throat and shifted on her feet, pleating her riding skirt with restless fingers.

"Taking a helping hand doesn't have to interfere with taking care of yourself."

"You're right, of course. I don't know where I got my stubborn streak. My momma always said I got it from my daddy. But I don't see it. My dad will hold his own when he thinks he's in the right, but he's the first that's willing to compromise when it's needed. Comes from being a politician, I suppose. Though he says there's a lot of them that would rather cut off their nose than compromise."

"Your dad's a politician?"

"Yes, a congressman."

"That Baylor." His eyes widened. "So, you're the senator from Missouri's daughter." Surprised recognition slapped him.

"Yes."

"I've heard of him."

"I'm not surprised. He's a mild-mannered man unless he runs up against injustice. He's a firebrand for the downtrodden." She laughed.

"I'm sure you're proud of him."

"Yes, I am."

He watched as her lips curved. Warmth and love for her father softened her features and lit her eyes.

Still smiling, she looked around. The tall building to the left of the telegraph office caught her eye. A drugstore with a wide window showed a little man bustling behind the counter, mixing powders.

"If you'll excuse me, I'm going to pop in here for just a minute and pick up shampoo." Sage pointed at the drugstore.

"I'll wait for you here." He propped himself against the outside of the building, his knee bent and his back and a boot heel pressed against the hard planks.

Two young women passed by giving him coy smiles and giggling. Both had dark ringlets of hair. One wore a pert lavender bonnet with a feather in it that fluttered when she laughed.

"Ladies." He tipped a black hat with a silver band on it.

They giggled harder, throwing flirtatious glances over slender shoulders.

Sage rolled her eyes and stepped inside.

Hawk could hear her clear voice asking for shampoo. A few minutes later she headed back out, carrying a brown paper bag.

A cowboy came swaggering down the street just as she stepped onto the sidewalk. Hawk hurried forward as she collided with the swaggering cowboy.

"Excuse me," she said, grabbing her package and straightening.

"Watch where you're going, lady." The man was about his age with a fancy black leather vest and a red bandana tied at a rakish angle. Thick black brows came down and he glowered at her. As the cowboy's gaze took her in, his expression changed. A hot feral light jumped in his eyes and he grabbed an arm to steady her, just as Hawk leaped forward and grabbed her other arm to keep her from falling.

"What have we here?" The cowboy tried to draw her closer, but Sage ground in her heels.

"Take your hands off me." Sage yanked at her arm to no avail and winced as fingers in black leather gloves dug in.

"Or what, pretty lady?"

Before she could respond, Hawk spoke. He didn't raise his voice. "Or I'll have to kill you."

The cowboy turned red-rimmed brown eyes on Hawk and inadvertently loosened his grip enough for Sage to wrench her arm away.

"You and who else?" the cowboy sneered. Brown hair stuck in disarray outside his hat. He would have been handsome if it hadn't been for the eager, hot light in his eyes and the feral smell emanating from his body. Like Hawk, he was dressed in black. Two pistols rode on his hips.

Tension crackled through Hawk's shoulders. He flexed them and emptied his mind. His lips formed a straight line. He shook his fingers and kept his muscles loose, ready for anything. His gaze never leaving the stranger in front of him.

Sage's wide-eyed stare skittered to Hawk.

"No one else is needed." Hawk put his hand on his gun. "Sage, go inside."

"Yeah, little lady. Go inside. I'll know where to find you when this is over." The hombre's lip curled in a sneer as his hungry gaze devoured her.

She ignored him and turned to Hawk.

"Hawk, it's not worth it."

"Hawk? You're the gunslinger? I heard tell you were seven foot tall and carried two pearl-handled pistols." The stranger's chin jerked up.

"You heard wrong. Though, you got the pearl-handle right. But I only need one pistol to take care of you."

"I've been hoping to run across you. I'm Jimmy Lee Jones. Heard of me?" An eager smile spread across the stranger's face and he shook out his hands, holding them over his pistols.

"Can't say as I have."

"Once I put you in the ground, people will hear of me soon enough."

"Hawk, please." She moved to Hawk's side.

He threw her an impatient look, but said, "What do you say, Jimmy Lee Jones? You want to apologize to the lady and live another day?"

"I want your glory and to get that I need to kill you."

"Back up, Sage," Hawk commanded.

"No. I won't have anyone die for me."

"Going to hide behind a woman's skirts, Hawk, or move this out to the street?"

Hawk gave her a quick look. She bit her lips together but couldn't keep the plead out of her eyes.

He gave an almost imperceptible sigh then leaped forward. His pointed, black-toed cowboy boot making contact with Jimmy Lee's crotch. The young gunslinger doubled over, his knees giving. Dust rose from the planks of the sidewalk as he dropped onto it and lay moaning.

Hawk grabbed him by his shirt front, pulled him up and gave him a clip on the jaw that shot pain from his knuckles to his elbow, then let him go. The man slumped, unconscious, back to the sidewalk.

"Pardon me." He pushed through the crowd of bystanders that had gathered round. Cutting a path for Sage.

"Thank you," Sage said as they stepped inside the telegraph office.

"You got a lot of your daddy in you, I'll say that."

"What do you mean?" She threw him a curious look.

"Avoid blood-letting at all costs." Frustration still roiled through him.

"You think pride is more important than getting yourself killed?" she replied hotly.

"I wouldn't have gotten killed."

"You don't know that."

He shrugged.

"Or killed somebody?"

"While I appreciate your sentiments and softer nature, you've just put off the inevitable. Now that I bested him, he's going to be gunning for me. Next time I might not see him coming."

She let that sink in. Mortified heat flooded her features.

"I'm sorry."

He gave her the easy smile that normally rode his face. "No need to apologize. You did what you thought was right. And that's all you can do. Now you better send that telegram."

"Right." Her skirt rustled as she whipped around and briskly strode to the counter. She spoke to a thin, balding man, with a no-nonsense manner. The clerk pulled out a sheet of paper and began to write.

Hawk turned his attention to the street. Wary. Watchful.

~*~

An hour later they were riding out of town. Around them clumps of buffalograss mingled with blue flowers and reddish-brown soil. The earth rising and falling, melding into craggy rock. As on the journey in, Sage's head swiveled back and forth, taking everything in. Her sea-gray eyes shining. She laughed and pointed at a leathery-looking creature with a long skinny tail that was disappearing down a short, steep rocky gorge. "What is it?" She leaned forward in her saddle, trying for a better look.

"An armadillo."

"What a charming fellow." She reined her horse and started after him.

"Where are you going?"

"I just want to see what's over the next horizon."

"Sagebrush more'n likely."

"What did you say?" She turned in her saddle.

Before he could respond, her horse stepped in a gopher hole and stumbled.

He thumped his mount's sides and the pinto shot forward. He reached her just as she managed to right the chestnut. Heat seared her face. "Stupid," she muttered.

"You or the horse?" Almost seeing her go under large hooves had unnerved him. Still, he should have held his tongue.

"What do you think?" she shot back taking the reins in a firm hand and straightening her spine.

"I'm just a hired hand. I'm not paid to think."

"I'll remember that." Her voice crisp, she urged her horse forward.

He followed then pulled up behind her when she stopped and straightened like a pointer, staring at a clear stream rippling over rocks and sparkling in the sunlight.

Drinking from it was Blue with a small band of mares.

She didn't hesitate. Putting heels to her mare's flanks she urged the horse down a small winding trail. Kicking up puffs of fine dirt and pebbles, her mare galloped down the gulley.

"Damn woman." He thumped his heels against his horse's flanks and raced after her.

Blue's head shot up and giving a ringing neigh, he galloped away, the small band of mares at his heels.

She reined in beside the creek and watched the band disappear.

He pulled up beside her.

Forgetting impatience and anger, she turned toward him, her face alight. "He's magnificent, isn't he?"

"Yes." But neither his mind nor his eyes were on the stallion.

"Did you hear that?" She looked around.

"What?" He gave himself a mental shake. Once again, he had to remind himself that you didn't go messing with anyone under Reuben Hayes' protection. Not to mention, she set off all sorts of warning bells. The kind that threatened a man's freedom. Instead of new cantinas and pretty senoritas, a man's thoughts turned to settling down. Something he wasn't near ready to do.

"Over there." She pointed to her left at a rocky outcrop and wrapping the reins loosely around the pommel, leaped out of the saddle, and trotted toward the sandstone crag with an animal-sized fissure in it.

Then he heard it too. Yipping. He straightened. "Get back in the saddle."

If she heard him, she paid no heed as she neared the arroyo's opening. Her boots leaving prints in fine red dirt.

"Oh, look."

Three fuzzy gray wolf pups came tumbling out of the crevice.

"Get back," he yelled, just before all hell broke loose.

Snarling, the mama leaped out of the fissure. Frightened, the chestnut reared and took off, her hooves pounding, growing distant as she galloped away until the sound died in the distance.

He whipped out his gun.

"Don't shoot," she screamed even as the wolf crouched.

Cursing, he shot over the wolf's head as it leaped. It yipped as the bullet hit the tip of its ear before ricocheting off the rocky outcrop. A rock, blasted from the bluff, catapulted straight at him. He ducked. The rough stone grazed his cheek as it flew in the air and finally landed in sagebrush.

"Run," he yelled, holding out his hand.

This time she followed instructions and came racing toward him, grabbed his hand and leaped up behind him.

"Heeya." He urged the pinto on as the wolf shook its head, taking a tentative step toward them.

The horse ran full out.

The pinto put a healthy distance between them, before Hawk reined him in to a canter.

"Hope we beat that chestnut to the barn," Hawk muttered.

"What did you say?"

Hawk tried to ignore her warm breath in his ear as she leaned closer to speak over the whistling wind.

"Reuben will skin me if he sees that horse come galloping in alone." Hawk feared no man. Could hold his own against anyone. But there was just something about Reuben Hayes that made him leery to ruffle the big man's feathers. The scars on his oversized knuckles for one thing and the comfortable way he wore his gun on his hip for another.

"Why? None of this was your fault."

He raised his voice so she could hear him. "He'd figure it was and he wouldn't be far wrong."

"I just don't understand the logic of the male animal." She lapsed into silence and he didn't break it.

The tension between Hawk's shoulder blades

lessened as they climbed the rise that led down to the ranch. They reached the crest and his shoulders tightened right back up as he saw Reuben riding hell for leather toward them. His leather vest flapping against his faded red shirt.

"Might as well get this over with," he muttered under his breath and nudged his pinto forward.

They were halfway down when Reuben reached them. Clots of dirt flew as the Appaloosa came to a stiff-legged halt.

"What the hell happened? The chestnut just thundered into the barn, covered in foam, the whites of her eyes showing."

He nudged his horse up next to Hawk. "Well?"

Gray eyes, like hurling spears, arrowed his own. Reminiscent of another pair of eyes, whose owner appeared to be using his back as a shield. An irrelevant thought rose unbidden. *If they aren't related, I'll eat my hat.*

"I ain't asking again." Reuben moved his horse closer till Hawk could feel the heat from the Appaloosa rising from his heaving sides.

Sage said nothing. No doubt struck dumb from the smoke spiraling from Reuben's ears and the fire in his eyes, putting Hawk squarely between a rock and a hard place. He couldn't very well tell what happened without getting that ire turned on Sage.

That the man had been scared right down to his boots for the young woman could not be denied. And like most men when frightened, turned the fear into anger. And boy oh boy, Reuben's rage was towering.

Hawk straightened his shoulders and gave Reuben a stoic look.

Reuben's face took on an unhealthy shade of red. He reached out, wrapped his fist in the neck of Hawk's shirt and lifted him out of the saddle, their faces inches apart. "I'm waiting." Hot breath, laced with coffee, fell on Hawk's face.

There was no help for it. He hoped to hell he didn't get his butt kicked. The big man had at least fifty pounds on him, with muscles hard as a boulder.

Reuben drew back one of those big fists. Hawk was hamstrung by the horse dancing under his legs and the woman behind him clinging like a leech. Nevertheless he tightened his free fist.

"It was my fault, Reuben." Sage pushed away from Hawk and straightened, raising her chin, even though it tended to wobble. Her eyes shot the same thunderbolts as Reuben's as she repeated, "My fault."

Hawk's breath whished out of his lungs, as Reuben released his grip on the neck of his shirt. Not that his face was what you'd call pretty, but he was partial to it and would just as soon not have it rearranged, especially his nose.

"Explain."

"I saw wolf pups and got off my horse to see them."

Reuben's eyebrows rose to his hairline and once again he rounded on Hawk. "And you let her?"

He opened his mouth then snapped it shut. What could he say?

"I jumped off before he could stop me. He told me to get back in the saddle then everything happened at once. The momma wolf came charging out of the crevice. My horse got scared and took off."

Reuben raised an eyebrow as he digested this. "What happened to your cheek?" he asked Hawk.

Hawk touched the jagged line of dried blood on his face. "Rock hit me when my bullet ricocheted off the arroyo.

"You missed?" Reuben's eyebrows that had went down rose again. "I thought you were some kind of hotshot with your pistol."

"I told him not to shoot her."

"And you listened to her?"

Hawk wisely kept his mouth shut. There was no way he was winning this one.

"And if that ghastly Jimmy Lee Jones shows up that will be my fault too." Sage threw herself back in the ring.

"There's more?" Once again graying eyebrows rose high.

Sage opened her mouth to explain but Reuben shot out an arm and interrupted. "I don't want to hear any more till we're home and I've had a whiskey." And on that note, he wheeled his horse and galloped off.

Later that evening when Hawk had a chance to explain, Reuben told him, "You should have killed him. But other than that, I guess you did the best you could given the circumstances. Shot the wolf in her ear instead of the heart huh?"

And Hawk knew that was as close to an apology as he'd get for nearly having the breath rung out of him and his face rearranged.

CHAPTER 5

Warm liquid rose in a rainbow arc of soapy water, and pots banged on the stove, as Soggy bustled around the kitchen.

Worn white curtains floated in the spring breeze as the first beams of sunlight streamed through the east window and warmed the back of Reuben's neck. He reached for the steaming cup of coffee in front of him and took a swallow. His features relaxed as the dark, hot liquid rolled down his throat and hit his breadbasket. He leaned back in his chair. "That's good coffee, Soggy."

"Of course, it is." The cook's chin went up and his chest swelled.

"Sit down and eat."

Soggy slapped down a couple of bowls of oatmeal, and thick slices of yeasty bread fried in butter, in front of Reuben and the place across from him on the long pine table. Boney hind end hit wood as Soggy dropped down across from his boss.

"Sage must be sleeping in." Reuben scooped up a spoonful of hot, thick oats that held a hint of cinnamon.

"Haven't seen her yet this morning, so I'd say so."

"Well, she had a pretty big day yesterday."

"That she did. Kind a nice having the young lady around, ain't it?"

"Yeah." Reuben stared at his oatmeal. How long would she stay before—like her mother—she'd head back East, and take his ole heart with her?

"We got her now. Let's not worry about the future."

"You read me like a book, don't you, ole man?"

"Who you calling old?"

"Must have been referring to myself since you work rings around me."

Soggy harrumphed.

Like an old married couple, they lapsed into comfortable silence. The only sounds, Soggy slurping his oatmeal and Reuben biting down on his fried bread.

The outside door slammed and boots tramped through the house to the kitchen. Hawk stopped in the entryway.

"Boss. Soggy."

"Hawk. Care for a cup of coffee?" Reuben raised his large ceramic mug.

"Depends." He stood with his hat in his hand.

"On what?"

"I was wondering if Sage was up yet?"

"Now why would you be wondering that?" Reuben's eyes narrowed.

"The chestnut's gone."

Soggy jumped to his feet and hurried down the hall. Minutes later he strode back in the kitchen, his features drawn.

"The bed's empty."

The blood drained from Reuben's head to pool in his toes, and the oatmeal and bread he'd ate moments before turned to a hard ball of worry in his stomach. He pushed to his feet.

"Her clothes are still in the closet, along with her carpetbag," Soggy said.

"So, she didn't head back in town. Where in hades would she go?" Reuben rubbed his forehead.

"You don't think she went to the old homestead, do you?" Soggy asked, his normally pugnacious features worried as he twisted the old white towel fastened around his waist with gnarly fingers.

"To my knowledge, she doesn't know where it's at. But it's a starting point, I suppose." He sighed heavily out of his nose.

"Hawk, saddle our horses. Then tell Billy to ride out and tell the others to keep an eye out for her. He'll know where everybody's at."

Hawk shoved his hat on his head and disappeared out of the house.

"You were saying earlier?" He raised his eyebrows at Soggy.

"Yeah," the older man responded glumly.

Reuben turned and strode out of the house. His heels clicked on the porch as he loped across it and went trotting down the steps just as Hawk came out of the barn leading the Appaloosa and his pinto.

Reuben strode to meet him, took the reins and threw himself into the saddle. He thumped the big horse's sides before Hawk had settled into the saddle. Dust flying from huge hooves, the Appaloosa tore down the lane.

It took them half an hour at a good gallop to reach the rundown cabin.

Bits jangled and the horses shook their heads and snorted, as the men reined in near the front of the log structure.

The door hung open. The glass in the windows long gone, their frames crumbling.

A corner of the roof sagged and a plank on the porch was missing, the steps rotted through. A wild rosebush near the porch spread its green leaflets attached to prickly branches in all directions, taller than a man.

There was no horse tied nearby. No footprints broke the dust on the porch.

"She's not here." Reuben's voice harsh as worry tracked up his spine. He turned in the saddle and asked without much hope, "Got any ideas?"

"Maybe."

"Let's hear it."

"She saw that wild stallion on the way to the ranch and lit up like a Christmas tree."

"Ole Blue?"

"Yeah."

"Take me there."

Hawk gave a clipped nod, nudged his horse with his heels and went galloping off. Reuben right behind him.

They rode north till they came to a rise where a

crystal-clear creek flowed below and bright blades of grass pushed through dark soil. An occasional blue flower sprinkled in the green.

A handful of mares pulled at tufts of new grass.

"Well, I'll be damned." Reuben stared in disbelief.

Several yards away, Ole Blue nibbled at something in Sage's hand then shook his head and snorted, his black mane dancing.

"Yeah." Hawk's jaw slack.

The wind shifted.

The stallion's head turned sharply as he caught their scent. He reared on his back legs causing Sage to jump backward, out of the way of massive, clawing hooves. Her heel caught and she sat down abruptly.

She threw her hands over her head as the stallion trumpeted and came down on all fours. Blue wheeled and took off at a dead run, away from Sage, the mares galloping behind him.

"Heeya." Reuben went racing down the rise, Hawk on his heels, clods and pebbles flying behind. Reuben raised his gun and shot it in the air scattering the herd, making sure none turned and headed in Sage's direction. In a nearby tree, a couple of blackbirds squawked and headed straight into the sky.

Reuben and Hawk's horses shot across the creek throwing up droplets of clear water that sparkled in the sun, wetting boots and hides.

They reached Sage at the same time. Hawk was off his horse and yanking Sage to her feet before Reuben could swing out of the saddle.

"Are you alright?"

"Yes," she said, her voice breathless.

Reuben clamped a hand on her shoulder and yanked her out of Hawk's grasp.

"Are you sure you're alright?" His chest caved in and pushed out, blowing heavily as a hard-ridden horse.

"Yes." She gave a shaky laugh.

The sound ripped through Reuben and rattled in his brain. She'd nearly died and she was laughing? Fear turned to fury. He forced his stiff fingers to open and dropped his hands, afraid he'd shake her till her teeth rattled.

"Where's your horse?" His tone sharp as he clenched and unclenched his big fists.

She gave him a wary look. Before she could respond, Hawk came forward leading the chestnut. Neither had noticed him slip away.

"Get on it and let's head home."

They mounted, crossed the stream and rode up the rise in silence.

When Reuben was sure he had himself under control, he said, "When we get back to the ranch house, pack your things. I'll take you in town to catch the stage."

"You want me to leave? Did you tell my mother to go too?" Her chin shot up, her features dead white.

He took the blow, his face stoic.

"I don't give my trust easily and when it's lost, it's gone."

"What are you talking about?"

"You know what I'm talking about."

"Because I rode out alone?" She stared at him in disbelief.

"There's a reason for me not wanting you to ride alone. There are all kinds of dangerous critters you could encounter. Four-legged and two-legged alike."

"I'm sorry. I shouldn't have gone without talking to you first." The words bit out. She stared straight ahead.

Apparently, apologizing didn't come any easier to her than it did to him.

"Though a gun wouldn't have helped me in this situation," she added.

"No, but having someone with you might have."

"I would have never gotten that close to Blue."

"Nor nearly got your skull caved in either," he snapped, getting mad all over again.

Hawk pushed between them.

"I'll teach her to shoot."

CHAPTER 6

Two sets of identical gray eyes narrowed on Hawk. Sage snapped her dropped jaw shut.

"I'm not staying where I'm not wanted." She flung her head up. Much like a prized filly, Hawk thought somewhere between bemusement and amusement.

Her chin was round where Reuben's was square, but they were sure jutted at the same stubborn angle.

Reuben took off his hat and rubbed his head then shoved it back on, his mad mostly over.

"It's not a matter of not wanting you. It's a matter of keeping you safe. If you want to stay and Hawk is willing to teach you to shoot, it would go a long way toward my peace of mind."

"And the trust?" She lifted her chin.

"Trust has nothing to do with wanting you to stay." He turned the Appaloosa. Horse and rider galloped back toward the ranch, leaving the two of them to follow.

"Stubborn," she muttered under her breath.

Hawk snorted.

"Did you say something?" Her eyes narrowed.

"No, ma'am."

"Hmm." She gave him a disbelieving look then fell

into a broody silence, broken only by the hooves of their horses as they trotted along, and an eagle that floated on a light breeze screeching overhead.

Finally, she said, "I better go make my peace."

"If you can hold onto your temper, he'll meet you halfway." *More like be putty in your slender, fine-boned hands.* But he wasn't about to give her that weapon to hold over Reuben's head.

"I don't have a temper." She flared up.

"I can see that." He gave her a knowing look.

She flashed a shamefaced grin.

"That's another thing my mother blamed on my poppa that I'll never understand. Unless he's talking politics, he's the most mild-mannered man you'd ever hope to meet."

Hawk forced his face to neutrality. Didn't allow his gaze to linger on Reuben's retreating back. There had to be blood there. They were too much alike not to be.

None of his business, he reminded himself and put heels to the pinto's flanks as they followed the Appaloosa's churning rump and swishing black tail across the plains.

Reuben stayed ahead of them for a good mile then slowed the Appaloosa to a trot. The two of them came galloping up on each side of him.

"I want to learn more about my roots." Sage reined in beside Reuben, bringing the chestnut to a trot.

"This is the place for it." One big paw wrapped around the reins of his horse, Reuben's other rested on his thigh.

"I think so too."

They looked at each other for a moment, then Reuben nodded. The tension broken.

"I also need to settle up with Mz. Krause at the boarding house. Could someone ride into town with me?"

"I settled up with her, but if you still want to go into town, Hawk can take you."

He was apparently back in good standing since he'd figured out where Sage was, Hawk thought wryly.

"How much?" Sage notched up her chin in a familiar gesture.

"How much what?"

"How much do I owe you?"

Hawk straightened, prepared for the storm. Just like spending time with two grizzly bears battling for supremacy, he thought. But moments later, realized he'd underestimated his wily boss.

"Well now, I don't need your money, girl." He shifted in the saddle and raised a hand before she could object. "But I understand needing to pay a debt. If you could give Soggy a hand now and then, I'd mightily appreciate it. He takes care of the house. The bunkhouse. And does the cooking with no assistance. I've tried to get him help. He refuses. And the man ain't getting any younger." For a moment, frustration flashed in Reuben's eyes. It was clear that he cared and cared deeply for his cook and friend.

"And you think he'll take it from me?" She arched a brow.

"I think you're smart enough to lessen his load and him not even know you're doing it."

"I'll see what I can do."

"I'd be in your debt."

"Don't worry, I'll figure out something."

Satisfaction flashed across the leathery, hard-edged face before being quickly masked.

Hawk shook his head in admiration. Reuben had avoided taking money from her without turning it into an almighty row. He'd gotten help for Soggy and with her spending more time under the cook's eagle eye it left less time for her to round up trouble which she seemed to find as easily as fleas a hound.

~*~

Crack. Squawk.

Hawk scratched his head. Sage had just managed to trim the tail feathers off a crow and take out the limb behind it.

The crow rose awkwardly into the air then let the soft blowing breeze carry it, its wings spread, its tail feathers floating softly to the ground. The branch passing the feathers and landing with a thump.

Crimson crept up Sage's neck and stopped only when it hit her hair line.

"If it wouldn't be presumptuous of me to ask, what were you aiming at?" He kept his face straight but had a problem keeping his lips from twitching.

She pointed at a branch higher up the old oak, loaded with tight buds of green, ready to unfurl.

"Try it again." He stood behind her, put his hands on her raised arms, determined not to be distracted by the clean scent of her or the warmth radiating from her skin. She wore a gray and blue plaid blouse and a split skirt. With the holster on her hip and brown leather cowboy boots, she looked every inch the frontier woman—until you saw her shoot. "Keep your eye on the target. Pull the trigger."

She jerked and pulled the trigger. The bullet shot through the air, missed the tree and caused a bird in a nearby pine to rise with a black flutter of wings, squawking.

"Try it again. This time don't jerk. Smooth and easy."

She took a deep breath, aimed and pulled the trigger. With a crack, the limb fluttered to the ground.

He dropped his arms and took a step back as she waved the Peacemaker, smiling, her eyes shining.

"I did it."

"Maybe you should holster the gun."

She laughed and shoved the Colt single-action, six-shot revolver into the worn leather holster on her hip. As she moved her hand, Hawk studied the plain-grain walnut handle.

"Who's K. W.?"

"I beg your pardon?"

"K.W." He pointed at the initials carved into the handle.

"Katherine Walsh. My mother." Color came and went in her face as she took out the gun and stared at the worn handle. A warm breeze lifted her hair and an eagle soared overhead.

"Interesting that he has her gun, isn't it? Just how close do you think Reuben and my mother were?"

CHAPTER 7

Rolled tobacco smoke rose in an acrid cloud that settled on the ceiling beams of the bunkhouse, tarred black from years of poker.

Hawk glanced at his pocket watch. Eight o'clock. He clicked it closed and shoved it into his vest pocket.

Most of the ranch hands, himself included, were crowded around an old round table, that wobbled if someone put too much weight on it.

A few lay on their bunks. One cowboy, sporting a healthy black beard, lay on his back, with one knee across the other, playing a mournful tune on his harmonica.

Billy kept looking at his cards and grinning like a hyena. Catching Hawk watching him, he tried to wipe the smirk off his face, but that grin just kept breaking out.

Hawk shook his head, his lips twitching.

Soggy looked at his hand and tossed it down in disgust. "I'm out." He got up and poured himself a cup of coffee that was strong enough to stand by itself.

"Pour me a cup and add a dollop, would you, Soggy?" Levi leaned back in his chair and scrubbed his leathery features with a callused hand.

"Me too, Soggy," Billy said.

"You can have the coffee."

"Aww, Soggy."

"Don't aww Soggy me, boy."

A cowboy wearing a green and blue plaid shirt strolled up to the stove and held out his tin cup. Soggy filled it up with the strong-smelling brew.

"I'm surprised no one has broke out the bottle before now." Hawk looked at his cards. Whatever the kid's hand, it couldn't beat a royal flush.

"The boss has strict rules about sobriety when you're working. If you want to get drunk as a skunk while you ain't working that's your business, but not on his time," Levi replied.

"And everybody abides by that?"

"The boss treats us fairly, we do the same."

"Makes sense to me," Hawk said.

"You want a mug of coffee and a dollop?" Soggy waved a banged-up pot at him.

"If it's all the same to you, I'll just take the dollop."

"Just remember what Levi said." Soggy grabbed a glass from the overhead shelf, blew the dust off and poured a splash of whiskey in it, carried it over and handed it to Hawk and thumped down Levi's coffee. His hand still on the cup he sniffed and frowned, his gaze drifting to the door. His eyes widened and his pupils dilated. He pointed and croaked out, "Fire!"

Curls of gray vapor slithered under the door, while small sparks of flame licked at the base. Hawk's chair smacked against the wood floor as he leaped to his feet and sprinted toward the door.

He grabbed the handle and yanked.

Nothing happened.

He grunted and pulled again.

The thick wooden barrier didn't budge.

Heels thumped and chairs squawked as the rest of the crew raced toward him.

"Door's jammed and there's smoke coming under it."

"Here let me try." Levi reached for the handle as small flames began to lick the bottom of the door.

Levi shook the door. "It's jammed alright."

Hawk grabbed a blanket from the nearest bunk and, wrapping it around his hand and arm, put his fist through the only window in the long cabin. Glass shattered in prisms of color.

The window was small and shoulder high. Hawk knocked out the remaining shards of glass sticking up from the base of the frame and leaped through it, his shoulders scraping against the edges, splinters pricking his arms.

He slid onto the ground, hands first, a sliver of glass imbedding itself in his palm. He raced toward the door as flames licked it. A chunk of wood jammed the door handle shut. Ignoring the flames and the heat from the handle, he pulled the wood out and threw open the door.

The men came tumbling out.

"Grab buckets and get water from the pump," Soggy yelled.

Billy raced for the pump, Levi at his heels. Soggy came huffing behind them.

Hawk beat at the flames with the blanket.

Reuben and Sage came tumbling out of the house. "What's going on?" he hollered.

"Bunkhouse is on fire, grab those buckets by the pump and start filling them up," Soggy bellowed.

Reuben and Sage jumped into action. When Billy reached the pump, Sage handed him a bucket. He passed it off to Levi, who handed it to Soggy. A brigade formed. Hawk took the bucket from a man named Slim and tossed it on the door now in flames. The blaze hissed and spit as water hit it. When Hawk whirled around, Slim took the empty bucket and handed him a full one, water sloshing over the sides. Then another and another till the door, and the wood surrounding it, was damp and smoldering. They threw several more buckets on for good measure, but by now the flame was out.

Hawk shook his hand as the pain and heat from grabbing the hot door handle made itself known.

Soggy noticed. He huffed over to Hawk and grabbed his hand.

Hawk winced and jerked it back. The abrupt movement ratcheting up the throbbing discomfort.

"Come to the house and let me see to that."

"Later. I'm going into town." The danger over, fury set in. He had a damn good idea who'd set that fire and jammed the door to the bunkhouse so they'd be toasted like burnt bread.

"You ain't going nowhere with that hand of your'n. And to my way of thinking till you get it seen to there ain't too much you can do with it."

Soggy notched his chin, his expression belligerent, his chest heaving and his lungs working like bellows. A smudge of soot on his forehead.

"Now let me see it."

Hawk rolled his eyes and held out his hand wishing for something to relieve the sting, like a stiff drink to toss back.

Soggy sucked in his breath.

Hawk glanced down. His palm had been branded with the door handle much like the steers that wore the marks of their ranch owners.

"Come with me." Soggy grabbed him by the arm.

Before he could comply or shake him off, Reuben threw down his bucket and came bulling through his men, Sage at his heels.

He stopped beside the two men.

"What the hell happened?" he demanded, fists on hips, eyes sparking.

"Somebody locked us in and set the door on fire. Hawk here jumped through the window and unlocked the door. Too bad he didn't have enough sense to use his vest to open the door instead of burning himself six ways to Sunday," Soggy said.

Sage shoved Reuben aside.

"Let me see."

"There's no need." But Hawk got no further as she grabbed his hand much as Soggy had then gasped in dismay.

"Come into the house. That needs treated."

"I'm going into town." Hawk jutted his chin at the same angle that Sage and Reuben's normally sat, the pain making him testy.

"Not till that hand is seen to."

She began tugging him toward the house.

"You think you know who did this?" Reuben fell in step beside him.

"I've got an idea."

Sage stumbled. Her face ashen in the moonlight.

"You think it was Jimmy Lee."

"I think I'm going to find out."

"Get your hand seen to and then I'll ride along with you. My ranch. My men." Reuben's voice left no room for argument. "Plus, I'm not sure how much good you'll be with that burned paw."

"I've got a left-handed holster in my saddle bag."

Reuben gave an abrupt nod and they strode toward the house.

They trooped in and headed for the small kitchen off the long dining area. A hard-back chair sat against the far wall, a small cutting table nearby. Soggy pointed at the chair and Hawk dropped into it and let his head fall back against the cool white-washed wall.

"What can I do?" Sage asked, her features strained. She still wore her split skirt and plaid blouse. That glorious chestnut hair loose from its moorings, catching the light and gleaming as Soggy lit a lamp.

"Pump me a bowl of cold water."

A small hand pump sat over the sink on the far side of the wall. An enameled, cast iron trough with a drain board beneath it. Reuben had told Hawk he'd rigged up cast iron pipes to drain water from the sink to outside the house where a yellow wild-rose bush flourished under the kitchen window.

Sage hurried to do as directed. Water splashed against the edge of the bowl as she pumped the handle up and down.

Soggy took the bowl and sat it in Hawk's lap.

"Put your hand in that."

The cold liquid soothed.

Soggy opened the pantry door and pulled out a bottle of amber-colored liquid and poured a healthy amount in a glass then thrust it at Hawk.

Hawk tossed back the whiskey. Between the cool on his hand and the burning in his belly, he felt a shade better.

"Break me off a piece of that aloe vera on the windowsill, will you, girl?"

She did as instructed.

"Now squeeze it over Hawk's hand."

Sage took a clean white towel and gently patted Hawk's hand then squeezed the plant's liquid onto Hawk's stinging paw.

He stared in bemusement at the top of her head bent over his hand, wanting nothing more than to touch the silk of her hair. Looking up, his gaze clashed with Reuben's whose narrowed eyes drilled him. The heat from his hand rose to the top of his head and he looked hastily away. The last thing he needed tonight was Reuben's wrath, which seemed barely held in check.

"Is that any better?"

"Actually, it is. Thank you." Getting his thoughts back on track, away from the dangerous area they were lingering in.

Soggy nudged her aside. Noticing the sliver of glass stuck in Hawk's palm, he plucked it out, then wrapped a clean bandage around Hawk's hand.

"Come back tomorrow and I'll change the bandage and put more aloe on your hand."

"Is that the plant you just had Sage dribble on me?"

"That's it."

"Where'd you learn about that? It seems to help." He flexed his fingers.

"From my mammy, who learned about it from her mammy."

"Well, I appreciate it."

He spoke to Soggy, but his eyes were on Sage, who gave him a tremulous smile.

"You still want to go in town?" Reuben cut in, his voice rough and impatient.

"I do. I just need to stop by the bunkhouse." His lips thinned.

"I'm sorry."

All eyes turned toward Sage.

"What are you sorry for?" Reuben asked. His hands in his pants pockets, he rocked on his heels.

"If it was Jimmy Lee, it's my fault that most of your men nearly died. I stopped Hawk from following through." She looked Reuben directly in the eye as she spoke, but couldn't keep the shudder from running through her body.

"Well as to that, Hawk has a mind of his own. He could have followed through on what needed done in spite of you."

She opened her mouth to protest, but Reuben waved it aside and continued, "Be that as it may, you see the good in people and that's not a bad thing, but out here we got more than our share of hombres that don't have a decent bone in their body. Sometimes you just need to temper your desire to do right by everyone to what needs done at the moment. You can't be soft and survive out here."

"That's pretty harsh."

"It's a harsh land."

"Maybe there's a spot to meet in the middle between harsh and what you consider soft."

"Maybe there is." He gave her a rare smile.

She smiled back.

He wheeled on his heel and looked straight at Hawk, the smile wiped off. "Let's ride."

Reuben and Hawk strode out of the house together.

"I'll saddle the horses and meet you in front of the bunkhouse."

Hawk nodded and they split off.

Hawk strode in the bunkhouse where the men were still milling around.

"Are you okay?"

"Thanks for getting us out of here tonight."

"Do you know who did it?"

"What did the boss have to say? Is he mad as hades?"

Questions flew fast and furious as Hawk opened the chest at the bottom of his bed, unbuckled his holster with his left hand, laid his gun on the bed and dropped the holster into the chest where brass clicked when it hit wood. Then he drew out his left-handed holster and awkwardly buckled it on.

"You heading to town?"

Before he could respond, Reuben stepped into the charred doorway, filling it, his shadow long and wide.

The men quieted.

"Tim. Joe. Tomorrow, you rebuild the door and frame."

"Will do."

"Sure thing, Boss."

He looked at Hawk.

"You ready?"

Hawk gave a short nod, dropped his colt into its holster and strode toward him. They left the building together.

The horses waited outside, tied to the hitching post.

Hawk gathered the reins, stuck his toe in the stirrup, and bouncing on the other foot, flung himself into the saddle.

Reuben leaped into the saddle, agile for a man of his size and age, and nudged the Appaloosa into a gallop. Hawk pulled alongside. The moon up. The stars bright, lighting the night sky, throwing a beacon on the ground that the horses loped over.

"So, you think it was this Jimmy Lee character?"

"It's a possibility. I embarrassed him and he's gonna want payback."

"Sage interfered with you finishing it?"

He didn't answer and instead asked, "So, you got

any other ideas of anyone who might want to finish off the crew?" Unwilling to place the blame on Sage. It had been his decision to let Jimmy Lee go, even if he knew at the time it was a mistake.

"Well, I've made my share of enemies, but nothing untoward over the last few months."

"We'll be finding out."

"Yeah," Reuben said in his rough, gravelly voice.

They lapsed into silence that lasted to Mobeetie. Most of the buildings dark, except for lights winking from swinging doors of saloons and the muffled sounds of a tinny piano from up the street as their horses clopped along.

Reuben reined in the Appaloosa in front of a seedy-looking building with peeling paint and a wooden sign that simply said SALOON.

"We'll start here." Reuben swung out of the saddle, wrapped the reins around the hitching post and strode to the door.

Hawk kicked his boot loose from the stirrup and, avoiding using his right hand, jumped down then tied the reins with his left.

He came to a stop beside Reuben, clean air replaced by the smell of stale beer and cheap perfume.

"You see him?" Reuben's gaze traveled the cramped room where half a dozen round tables held a handful of cowboys, one with his head on the table snoring. The gray hair on his forehead, visible under a brown cowboy hat, lifted with each noisy breath. Another couple of men leaned at the bar.

Hawk took a long, careful look around.

"He's not here."

They moved on to the next bar.

Jimmy Lee wasn't there.

Irritation and nerves crawled through Hawk's system. He had no doubt Jimmy Lee was responsible for the near disaster at the ranch, but there was nothing saying he didn't jump on his mount and head out of Texas. It would be the smart thing to do. But what little he knew of Jimmy Lee didn't give him much reason to believe thinking was Jimmy Lee's strong suit.

Their heels clomped against the sidewalk planks to a backdrop of cicadas, and a tinny-sounding piano coming from the Red Horse Saloon.

Reuben rammed into him as he stopped abruptly his hand on the swinging door. The smell of smoke and yeasty liquid filling his nostrils. Only this smoke brought the comfort of cigars and not the terror of death.

Hawk's eyes narrowed. Jimmy Lee sat at a scarred round table, a whiskey in one hand, cards in the other, and a girl dressed in an emerald satin dress, with thin straps, tightly fitting her bosom and waist, sitting on his lap. He wore a satisfied grin.

As if drawn by the force of Hawk's stare, he raised his head. His eyes widened and his jaw dropped. Whiskey sloshed on the table as his glass slipped through his fingers. Then a slow, satisfied smile spread across his features.

"Sorry, darlin." He nudged the girl off his lap and stood.

"You come to try your gun hand after all?"

Savage anticipation rushed through Hawk. His blood pumped through his system leaving his nerve endings tingling. He started forward. A hard hand on his shoulder stopped him in midstride.

"That him?" Reuben's raspy voice rougher than usual.

"Yes, and I'd say the expression on his face when we walked in is as good as an admission," Hawk ground out between clenched teeth.

"Yeah." Reuben gave him a shove that sent him into a nearby table. Two men cussed as their drinks spilt and ran in a golden flow of liquid off the table and onto the floor.

Reuben strode right up to Jimmy Lee till they were toe to toe.

"You Jimmy Lee?"

"What's it to you, ole man?"

Yup. Nothing but air between that hombre's ears. Hawk shook his head, crossed his arms and settled back to watch the show. He could almost feel sorry for Jimmy Lee. Almost.

Silence fell. Men leaned in eagerly. Ready for some entertainment on an otherwise dull night.

"Like to play with matches, boy?"

"I don't know what you're talking about and quit calling me boy."

Reuben grabbed him by the front of his shirt and twisted his fist in it.

"Well then, how about you yellow, cowardly, son of a jackal."

"Now just a—"

Whatever else Jimmy Lee was about to say was cut off by a big fist that landed between his eyes.

He went down without a sound, except the thump when he hit the floor and the rattle of a nearby table.

"Get up." Reuben leaned over him. When there was no response, he hauled him to his feet. Jimmy Lee's eyes opened. Reuben hit him again. Jimmy Lee's eyes rolled back and he slumped to the floor, arms and legs extended.

"You're going to make it kinda hard for me to draw down with him if he can't stand on his feet, let alone pull his gun from his holster." Hawk's lust for blood, while still riding high, had leveled off with each thump of Reuben's fist between Jimmy Lee's eyes.

"You got a bum hand."

"My left works just fine."

"Hmm." Reuben's expression skeptical.

A long lanky man got up from a back table and ambled toward them. A tin star pinned to a tan vest.

"John." Reuben nodded to him.

"Got a problem here?"

"This low life tried to burn down the bunkhouse with my men inside it."

"Is that right?" For a moment, brown eyes in a craggy face turned steely.

"Want me to lock him up? Justice Death is riding circuit this month and will be in next week."

Justice Death's actual name was Horace Jackson but he'd been nicknamed Justice Death because of the number of hangings he'd authorized.

Reuben studied Jimmy Lee, blood running from his nose and drool from his lips. The big man's fists clenched then relaxed.

"Works for me."

Hawk made a sound of protest deep in his throat. Reuben had at least got to work off his aggression with a couple of well-placed hits. His blood still roweled and fury choked him.

"I know how you feel. But hang'n is a whole lot more uncomfortable than a bullet that ends your life in seconds."

"Remind me never to piss you off."

The marshal broke in. "I've got to get my cuffs. Stuck 'em on Shorty when he took a swing at ole Gus who accused him of cheating at cards. Gus never was a good loser. Guess it's Shorty's lucky night."

The marshal meandered toward a table in the back of the room.

"He ain't going nowhere. Let's get a beer." Reuben elbowed through the crowd, heading toward the bar.

"Hi there, handsome." The young woman who'd been sitting on Jimmy Lee's lap came sashaying toward Hawk, taffeta skirt swishing, two curlicues of brassy blonde hair bouncing around her face as she moved.

"Look out," someone yelled.

Hawk whirled. Jimmy had drawn his gun and had it pointed at Reuben's back. Fast as lightning, Hawk drew and fired.

A pop sounded. Smoke rose. The gun fell, from Jimmy's fingers. His eyes rolled back. His head dropped to the floor. He'd drawn his last breath.

Both the marshal and Reuben came plowing through the crowd. The marshal reached him first, cuffs dangling from one hand, gun in the other.

"What happened here? I told you I was taking him in."

A scrawny little man with a full white beard spoke up. "I saw everything, Marshal. That there hombre had pulled his gun and had it aimed at Reuben's back. This young feller saved his life."

Reuben reached Hawk's side.

"What happened?" he demanded, staring at the dead man at his feet.

"Appears this young man saved your life," the marshal said.

"Can't figure out why he was aiming at you instead of me. Seems he prefers to shoot a man in the back," Hawk said.

"Looks like my debt to you is mounting."

Hawk shook his head.

"You look familiar," the marshal cut in. "What's your name, son? You ain't on any wanted posters are ya?" John asked, only half-joking.

"Name's Hawk and no I'm not on any wanted posters."

The marshal straightened, no longer smiling, his face hard.

"I've heard of you and I'd be obliged if you stay out of my town."

"John, Hawk works for me. I'll vouch for him."

"Reuben, he may be clean as a whistle, but he's

going to attract anyone within a hundred miles trying to make a name for himself or add a notch to his gun."

"I've had my share coming after me."

"So I've heard," John said his voice dry.

"A man should be judged on his actions, not others' actions."

The marshal mulled that for a moment then turned to Hawk. "You just make sure and keep your nose clean in my town. Got that?"

"I won't start anything, but I sure won't promise to walk away if someone else does."

"Now ya see? That's exactly what I'm talkin' about. But give it your best shot, will ya?"

"That I can promise to do."

"I didn't mean that literally." The marshal gave him a leery look.

"Neither did I." Hawk flashed him a grin.

"That's all I can ask." He swiveled to two young bucks gaping at the dead body. "Harold. Jonas. Help me get this carcass out of here and to the undertakers."

They each grabbed a boot and headed for the door. The marshal behind them.

"Night, John," Reuben called.

John raised a hand in the air, but didn't look back.

"Let's get that beer." Once more Reuben shoved through the crowd, Hawk right behind him.

"Two beers, Joe," he called to the bartender.

Joe poured them from the tap and slid them down the bar, the liquid still foaming.

Hawk took a deep gulp then wiped the foam from his mouth with the back of his hand. "I could always leave you know."

"You turning tail and running?" Reuben leaned an elbow on the bar, facing Hawk.

"I'm trying to do the right thing," Hawk said through clenched lips.

"Maybe the right thing is to stop selling your gun to the highest bidder and let that reputation die away."

"Did you know about my reputation when you hired me?" Hawk tipped his glass, studying the waves of gold liquid sloshing back and forth.

"I did."

"And you offered me a job anyway."

"I make my own decisions and they aren't based on hearsay.

"You've saved Sage's life and now you've saved mine. It would take a whole lot more than having a reputation for a fast gun to get me to ask you to leave. As far as I'm concerned, the matter's closed."

CHAPTER 8

"Your shooting must be improving, I ain't seen no crows missing tail feathers flying around." Reuben took a big bite of a hot yeasty roll.

"Good rolls, Soggy." He gave a nod to Soggy, half-hidden behind the mass of colorful wild flowers that sat in the middle of the table in a cracked ceramic pitcher. No doubt gathered by Sage. He'd never known Soggy to bother with flowers before. Glancing out the west window, he saw the color change in the sky. Pinkie-gray replacing blue. Nearly time to light the lamps.

Sage shot Hawk, who'd been invited to dinner, a hot look then grinned and shrugged. "I think so."

Reuben arched thick, winged eyebrows at Hawk.

"She's got a good eye and an easy finger on the trigger."

Before Reuben could respond someone hammered at the door.

"I'll get it." Soggy pushed away from the table. On permanently bowed, skinny legs, he strode out of the room and headed for the door.

Muffled voices carried into the dining room.

The door slammed and a moment later Soggy

stood in the doorway, his face white. He twisted the flour sack tied around his waist.

"Someone to see you." He looked straight at Reuben.

For his cocksure cook to be shaken was a rarity. Without asking questions, Reuben threw down his napkin and shot to his feet. He tromped out of the room and flung open the door.

Pacing on the porch, his heels clumping in rapid clips, stood the honorable Senator James Baylor.

Reuben's breath lodged in his lungs. The skin around his skull tightened like he was wearing a hat several sizes too small. The pressure in his head shrieked for relief.

The two men stared at each other. Sizing each other up, taking in the toll that the years had wrought on the other. James Baylor had a healthy sprinkling of silver in his hair and wrinkles around the eyes, but still as tall and gangly as ever. If the man hadn't married the only woman he'd ever loved, they'd probably be friends.

"James."

"Reuben."

"Are you here to take Sage home?"

"She's here then?"

"Yes."

"I came to reassure myself she arrived safely."

"Didn't she send you a telegram?"

"Yes, but it was rather vague. And I wanted to make sure she was alright. May I come in?"

His heart pounding, Reuben stepped back, and

waved the senator in. He hadn't known she existed for eighteen years and he didn't intend to give her up without a fight. But how in hell did one fight a pacifist? His fists and six-gun wasn't the answer.

"Who was it, Soggy?" Reuben heard Sage ask as they reached the eating area.

Soggy didn't respond.

Reuben and Baylor stopped in the entryway.

Sage glanced up. Her eyes lit and she leaped from her chair, with enough force to send it clattering to the floor, and ran into her dad's arms.

"Daddy, what are you doing here?"

The senator held her close, closed his eyes and breathed her in. Then pushed her away and looked at her. "You're a sight for sore eyes. After I got your telegram, I wanted to make sure you were okay." And bring you back home lay heavy and unspoken in the air.

Reuben waited for Baylor to ask Sage why she came here, but the question didn't come. He guessed the seasoned campaigner would wait and ask the question when it was least expected.

"As you can see, I'm fine."

"Senator, would you care for some vittles? Soggy's outdone himself tonight. I think we've even got a cherry pie for dessert."

"You won't catch me turning down one of Soggy's famous desserts." He clasped his hands then rubbed them heartily.

"I'll get you a plate." Soggy pushed back his chair.

"I'll get it, Soggy," Sage said.

"Sit. Sit." He tromped toward the kitchen.

Baylor pushed in Sage's chair then sat down across from her.

Reuben dropped into his seat as Soggy came back with plate, silverware and a big white mug filled with coffee that he plopped in front of the senator, sloshing dark liquid on to the table.

"Thanks, Soggy."

The cook grunted and dropped into his chair.

"So, Senator, how'd you get to Texas from St. Louie? Train then stage?" Reuben asked.

"That's right. Took the Santa Fe to Dodge City and from Dodge the stage."

Baylor reached for the plate of pot roast that Reuben thrust at him. "Looks like you've made a real success of this place. What's going on in the ranching industry?" The senator passed on the platter and thumped a healthy spoonful of steaming potatoes with the scent of butter and heaven rising from them onto his plate then passed them to Reuben.

"We're doing okay. You ever heard of Brandon Wade of the Silverhills' Ranch?"

The senator narrowed his eyes and wrinkled his forehead in thought then snapped his fingers. "I think I met him once. Handsome fellow. Has a way with the ladies?"

"That would be Brandon." Reuben threw back his head and laughed.

"Anyhow, he's developed a new breed of cattle called Herehorns. I plan to purchase a handful from him and improve my herd." The tight skin around

Reuben's shoulder blades relaxed a bit as he talked about his ranch. He loved the ranch, considered it a wild and willful mistress, but worth every minute of trouble she cost him.

The senator swallowed a mouthful of potatoes then asked, "Herehorns. What's that?"

"A mix of Herefords and longhorns. They've got the hardiness of the longhorn mixed with a better quality of meat from the Herefords."

"Sounds like he's pretty forward thinking."

"He is."

"So, what have you been doing since you've been here, love?" The senator turned his attention to Sage.

"I'm learning to shoot."

"Are you now?"

"Yes, on momma's old gun."

Her father looked at her in silence.

"How did you figure that out?" Reuben asked her, reaching for his coffee.

"The initials on the handle."

"Smart as a whip." He shook his head in admiration.

"She got it from her mother," Baylor said shortly.

"I never doubted it," Reuben returned.

The two men glared at each other. The temperature in the room cooling.

Sage glanced from one to the other, her forehead corrugating, her eyes narrowing.

"I'll get the pie." Soggy tossed down his napkin and headed for the kitchen, swaying from side to side with his bandy-legged gait.

"I'll help."

Sage pushed up and followed Soggy out.

"Want to grab a whiskey and move to the porch while they're fussing over the pie?"

"Yes."

The two men rose.

"Hawk?" Reuben asked.

"Go ahead. I'll help Soggy and Sage pick up the dishes."

Reuben gave him a brief clip of his chin, appreciating his diplomacy.

He strode into the study and came back with three whiskey glasses. He thumped one down in front of Hawk.

"For the pain."

"Appreciate it. Should I get one for Soggy?"

"Soggy has his later in the evening.

"Shall we?" Reuben handed a glass to Baylor and they stepped onto the porch. Holding their glasses, they stood on the veranda watching the sun set in a tangerine ball of glory. The red sky, reflecting the sun's splendor, turned Reuben's little piece of Texas into a swatch of heaven, hiding the rough and underscoring the glory.

Reuben gulped his whiskey in one swallow. Needing the burn to the throat and heat to the belly. "Did you know?" The words erupted as hot as his throat.

"Do you think Katherine would have married me without telling me?"

"So, she knew when she left?" Reuben's hand

tightened around his glass. He forced his tight fingers to loosen and set it down before he shattered it.

"No. It was several weeks before she figured it out."

"Why didn't she come home? Or send for me? I would have come for her in a heartbeat."

"She said you told her if she left not to bother to come back."

"She'd just ripped my heart out. All I had left was my pride. How could she think I wouldn't acknowledge my own child?" The wound Katherine had made when she left had never completely healed. Now the scab was ripped off and bleeding. He swore under his breath. He hated being vulnerable. Had always prided himself on being able to take on anything. Anything except Katherine Walsh. Why hadn't she told him? Did she hate him that much?

"I've never understood the workings of a woman's mind. Especially Katherine's." The senator gave a helpless shrug of his shoulders.

Reuben forced the pain back into the dark hole it had seeped out of and rubbed absently at an old wound on his right thigh, courtesy of an Apache arrow.

"You've done a fine job raising her."

"I couldn't love her more if she was my own flesh and blood. What do you intend to do?" The question abrupt.

Maybe the senator was fighting his own demons.

"Nothing. She's a guest of an old family friend." The words were offered in a raspy, calm voice, only the white knuckles and tic in his jaw belied the neutrality of the statement.

"She's going to figure this out you know. As you said earlier, the girl is smart as a whip. You best be prepared for whatever it is you're going to say."

"I won't lie to her."

"Never expected you to. What brought her out here anyway?"

"Katherine left me a letter."

"Oh." The word spoke volumes. "She loved me you know."

"Then you were a lucky man."

"But never like she loved you." He turned and strode back into the house. A dignified man with streaks of silver in his hair.

"Damn." Reuben stared into the sunset, for once the brilliant colors lost on him as he pulled together the tatters of his heart.

CHAPTER 9

Breaking dawn.

He rolled out of bed, threw on his clothes and opening the bedroom door breathed in a scent that enticed him more than leather, hay or horses.

Following the rich, nutty aroma of fresh coffee, Reuben clomped his way into the kitchen and grabbed up the blue, cracked ceramic mug sitting by the granite coffee pot and poured himself a cup, raised it and gulped. Hot caffeine rolled through his system and righted his world.

"Mornin'."

Stirring a mix of flapjacks, Soggy grunted.

Cup in hand, Reuben stepped onto the porch. A measure of peace seeped through him as he watched the changing pinks and reds of the sky as they slowly settled into blues, while horses snorted and neighed in the corral. A light wind carried the subtle scent of fresh, green, and wild roses that were planted at the side of the porch. He enjoyed their fragrance, but he'd let himself be hanged before he admitted it. Most folks thought him cold and unfeeling, and that was just fine by him. His reputation had a way of keeping would-be troublemakers at bay.

"Kinda surprised the senator spent the night."

Soggy stepped out onto the porch, rubbing his hands on the worn towel tied around his scrawny waist that emphasized the pooch of his belly.

"You invited him."

"You should have."

"Yeah."

"Why didn't you?"

He shot his cook a look that withered most folks but never fazed Soggy.

"You got to get over it. She married him. It's over and done with. Nineteen years is enough time to brood. It's time to move on."

"Aren't your flapjacks burning?"

"Yeah." Soggy rushed back into the house. The clomp of his heels growing faint, then disappearing, as he vanished into the kitchen. Reuben tossed out his rapidly cooling coffee and followed Soggy inside.

James Baylor stood in the kitchen, his back to the door, staring out the window and sipping on a cup of Soggy's fine coffee. The frisky wind pushed against the curtains that fluttered and revealed a frame that needed a fresh coat of paint. Baylor wore a pair of jeans and a green shirt the color of his daughter's namesake and looked at home in the comfy kitchen right down to the soles of his boots.

Soggy stood in front of the black, cast-iron wood-burner flipping flapjacks.

"I'm not sure your constituents would recognize you."

"Morning, Reuben. There's nothing like a Texas sunrise is there?" The senator turned and held out his hand.

Reuben took it. The senator's hand smooth against Reuben's calluses. "No, Senator. There ain't." Soggy's admonishment on his manners still ringing in his ears, he added, "Did you sleep okay?"

"Like a baby."

Reuben sensed her before he caught her particular fragrance, verbena, or heard the sharp click of her heels. It had been that way with her mother too. Something inside him just knew when she was there.

"Daddy." She rushed into Baylor's arms.

For a moment, the senator drew her close. Love in his smile.

Reuben's hand tightened briefly on his cup. The love was a good thing. He wouldn't have wished anything else for her. Still, it was hard not to have regrets.

His gaze clashed with Soggy who was watching him steadily.

"Better watch those flapjacks, old man." Reuben straightened.

"Who you calling old?" Soggy drew himself up and stuck out his chest like an irritated bantam rooster.

"Good morning, Reuben. Good morning, Soggy." Sage laughed, left her father's arms and went unerringly to the cabinet for a coffee cup.

The door banged, footsteps sounded, and Hawk stuck his head in the doorway.

"Good morning," Hawk said to everyone in general but his eyes lighted on Sage before they skittered away.

Becoming color rose in her cheeks.

"I came to see if Sage was ready for her shooting lesson." He stood with his hat in his hand, his piercing blue eyes once more fixed on Sage.

"Good timing on your part. Sit down and have some breakfast." Reuben motioned toward the table.

"Those flapjacks do smell mighty good." Hawk pulled out a chair and sat down as Soggy passed out plates of flapjacks and Sage the silverware. He hopped to his feet and pulled out her chair when she had finished.

"Thank you. I'm not sure about the lessons. It depends on Daddy's schedule."

She glanced inquiringly at her father.

"Go ahead. I thought I'd tag along with Reuben and see the ranch if that's alright with him."

"No problem at all." Reuben hid his surprise.

"When are you going back, Daddy?" Sage reached for the pitcher of warm syrup.

"In a hurry to get rid of me?" he teased.

"You know better."

"A day or two, if Reuben will have me. Then I need to get back to the capital."

Soggy gave him a fierce frown. Reuben shoveled a mouthful of warm flapjacks into his mouth and masticated before he could tell the senator not to let the door hit him on the way out. Though if it meant more time with Sage, he'd put up with the devil himself, which the senator wasn't. He'd just married the woman Reuben loved.

What about you?" the senator asked casually, but

his eyes were intent and his body perfectly still.

"I guess that depends on how long Reuben will put up with me."

Reuben swallowed his flapjacks and said, "You're welcome to stay as long as you like." Then went back to eating.

When he'd shoveled in the last mouthful, Reuben stood and threw down his napkin.

"You ready?"

The senator took one last bite, wiped his mouth, and pushed to his feet.

"Ready." He turned to the cook. "That was mighty good, Soggy."

The cook nodded.

Baylor kissed his daughter on the forehead then turned to Hawk. "I expect you to take good care of her, young man."

"That's my intent, sir."

"See that you do."

Sage rolled her eyes.

"Bye, Daddy. Reuben."

The men headed out the door.

Reuben stopped on the porch.

"Billy," he cupped his hands and called to the young man walking past the corral.

"Yes, sir."

"Saddle a horse for the senator." The Appaloosa, already saddled and waiting for Reuben, stood at the hitching post, stomping its hooves and swishing its tail.

"Yes, sir."

Billy disappeared into the stable. A few minutes later the two men were mounted and heading north.

"Where we going?" Baylor asked, as he sat stiffly in the saddle, his knees locked, one hand on the reins, one on the horn.

"Loosen your reins a bit. You'll both get along better," Reuben said, observing the bay's tendency to toss her head and sidle.

The senator did as directed. "It's been a while. I usually take a buggy or a horsecar."

"It'll come back to you. How long did you say you were planning on staying?"

"A day or two. I can move in town if you like."

"You're welcome to stay at the ranch." He couldn't quite keep the grudge out of his voice.

"Listen, Reuben, this is a bit awkward for both of us, but we're going to have to find a way of patching up our differences or this is going to explode in our faces."

"I've got nothing against you personally." Again, the grudge was in his voice, but he was a man who spoke his mind, not pussy-footed around the situation because of social niceties. It didn't sit well.

"But I married the woman you loved and raised the daughter you didn't know about."

The sun scuttled behind a cloud and thunder rumbled in the distance. Looked like a pop-up was gonna be on them. Maybe that was why his skin rubbed tight against muscle and nerve.

"That pretty much sums it up."

"I'd do it again." His long, thin face solemn, the

Senator turned his head to look directly into Reuben's eyes. Something Reuben respected along with the frank speech. The bay apparently didn't and chose to skitter at the thunder and almost unseated the senator.

Reuben reached out a hand but the senator righted himself. Reuben nodded his approval.

"You did a right fine job of raising Sage. That I can appreciate." He heaved a sigh that rumbled in his barrel-sized chest then reached out his hand. "It's time to let bygones be bygones."

The senator took it and gave it a firm shake then straightened in his saddle while the thunder continued to rumble in the distance. "Where we headed?"

"North pasture. There's a mountain cat in the area that's been picking off the calves and the sickly cattle. The sickly cattle I don't begrudge it, but the calves I do."

The senator nodded then said, "What can you tell me about that young man?"

"That he saved Sage's life twice now."

"And that's good enough for you?"

"It isn't for you?"

"I appreciate that of course. He looks like a gunman."

"You're in Texas." Reuben snorted.

"You know what I mean. What is it about him that you like so much?"

"He reminds me of me." Reuben swayed easily in the saddle. His horse, unlike the bay, oblivious to the thunder as it trotted along, its hooves squishing sprigs of green that popped back up behind it. And while he was as comfortable on his horse as he would be in an easy chair, he couldn't shake the unease that rode beside him.

"Well now, Reuben," the senator drawled. "I got to say, he's a might prettier than you are."

A surprised chuckle rumbled in Reuben's chest and just like that the ice was broken.

"That he is. Haven't known him long and he does have a checkered past, but my gut tells me he's solid."

"I guess that will have to be good enough for me. I just don't want to see her hurt."

"Well now. I wouldn't worry about that. He knows his life wouldn't be worth a plug nickel if he was crazy enough to do that."

"I'm afraid young men don't think with their heads but parts lower."

Reuben recalled the wild, tumultuous rush of blood that roiled hot through his system like a raging river.

"Yeah," he said glumly and fell silent, wondering if those feelings would have continued into middle age if Katherine had stayed. He'd had plenty of women since she'd left him. But it was release pure and simple. They'd heated his blood but none had touched his heart.

As they rode under a majestic old oak aflush with spring green, a startled red-wing blackbird flew almost under the senator's nose. He gave a violent start that spooked the horse. Baylor got him quickly under control but still took a superstitious look around.

Reuben's grin at the senator's reaction slid off his face and he tapped his thigh thoughtfully with the big square hand that rested on his denim pants. The senator seemed as jumpy as he was.

Reuben minded his own business and expected everyone else to do the same. Still and all the senator was his guest. And if the senator had a problem that meant he could have a problem as well.

"Want to tell me what's going on, James?" Reuben took a long look around. He covered his eyes with his hand, thinking he saw a rider in the distance but with the gray and a fog rolling in it was impossible to tell.

"Just a little jumpy I guess."

"So, I see. The question is why."

"Politicians always make enemies."

Saying nothing, Reuben waited, the only sounds breaking the silence, the screech of an eagle soaring on a cantankerous wind and the muffled clip-clop of hooves as the horses loped along.

Finally, the senator said, "Someone seems to have taken issue with my anti-lynching bill."

"You'd probably be lynched for suggesting it out here." He'd strung up more than one cattle rustler himself.

The senator shook his head. "You're a strong man, but you'd be sickened, Reuben. So much hate for folks that don't look like us. Ever seen a child lynched?"

Reuben said nothing but a spurt of acid burned in his gut. Some things went beyond wrong.

"I did and I couldn't stop it. Couldn't turn the mob. I vowed nothing like that would happen on my watch again."

"Care to elaborate?"

"There was this black child—"

"I got that. What makes you think someone has taken exception to your bill?" He twisted in the saddle, checking his surroundings. The senator's unease hiking up his own. He still couldn't see anything in the gray and the thick. If it didn't lift pretty quick, they'd head back. He trusted if it was this overcast Hawk had given up on the shooting lesson and taken Sage back to the ranch.

"I get the occasional hate mail. Lately, there's been some death threats thrown in and a couple of weeks ago, someone tried to knife me."

"Have you told Sage?" Reuben straightened in the saddle, frowning.

"No and neither will you. I don't want her worrying."

"Your choice."

"You don't approve?"

"Doesn't matter whether I do or not. Anybody know you're here?"

"I don't know. I've tried, but it's hard to keep a lid on my movements. Those reporters even comment on the color of my socks." The senator shook his head.

Reuben let out a short bark of laughter. The men more at ease with each other than they'd been since the senator's arrival.

"We'll keep an eye out. Maybe, given the fact

that someone has been taking potshots at you, we better head back. Sage would never forgive me if I let something happen to you."

"I didn't come here to hide out, Reuben, nor to have your six-gun protect me. Now let's go find that cat." The senator clucked to his horse and gave it a light kick in the ribs and headed for the arroyo in the distance. The sandstone usually orange and brown now gray in the gloom.

Reuben gave a short jut of his chin and started after the senator and began to see what Katherine had seen in him. He might be mild-mannered and easygoing but the man had backbone and if there was one thing Reuben admired, it was backbone. He lifted the Appaloosa into a lope and caught up with the senator as the fog lifted off the ground, still hanging in the crags of the canyon.

"Looks like the fog may be burning off. We might see your cat yet." The senator looked around.

Reuben did the same, watching the fog lift in an upward spiral. As the fog rose, he caught a flash of light and heard a distant boom. A sound as familiar as the snort of a horse.

"Look out." He dove onto the senator. Throwing them both to the ground as a bullet whined and bone-grinding pain tore through his left arm.

Whinnying, the horses took off.

"Stay down." With a grunt, he rolled off the senator and reached for his gun. He stood up and began firing in the direction the gunfire had come from. A bullet hit a bush nearby causing it to splinter in all directions. He continued to fire hot lead.

As he shot his last bullet and reached for the bullets on his belt, an hombre fell in slow motion from the top of the arroyo. A dark vest flapped, a tan hat fell off and floated in the wind beside him, hitting moments after the body. A cloud of dust rose as the shooter hit the ground.

The senator scrambled to his feet.

"Are you alright?" Reuben asked, striding toward the hombre who'd put a bullet in him.

"Better than you," the senator retorted, stretching out his legs and catching up with Reuben.

"You got me there." He fought back a grimace as torn flesh complained.

"You need to get that seen to."

"Let's see who was shooting at us then we'll head back to the ranch and Soggy can patch me up." Reuben unknotted the red bandana around his neck, then used his teeth and good hand to tie it on his arm to staunch the bleeding.

"Here, I can do that." The senator whipped off the bandana that Reuben had clumsily tied on. Folded it, then tied it back on the wound.

"I believe that's what I just did."

"After a fashion." With determined strides, the senator headed toward the downed shooter.

Reuben shrugged and followed. He caught up as the senator stopped and studied the body lying face down in the dirt and gravel. Reuben toed him over.

"Recognize him?"

"No, but then again his face isn't what it was a few

minutes ago."

Blood streamed from the hombre's nose and mouth. Various abrasions and dust covered his features.

Reuben looked at the Winchester repeater still clutched in the shooter's hand and the .44 caliber Remingtons strapped to his hips. He pulled the repeater from lifeless fingers and examined it. The hombre had meant business.

"Let's get back to the ranch." Reuben gave the lifeless form one last look then turned on his heels.

"And how do we do that?" The senator looked around. The horses gone.

Reuben put his fingers between his lips and gave a piercing whistle.

A whinny sounded and hooves thumped against shale as the Appaloosa came galloping back. The bay sauntered behind him, her cornsilk-colored mane flowing as she shook her head.

"You've got the touch," the senator said admiringly.

"Nope just a good horse. Katherine was the one that had the touch. How did she ever survive in the city?"

"I've got a place in the country. Bought it for her. Isn't much. Small and nothing fancy, but she kept her horses there. An old couple lives there for room and board. When the walls closed in, she'd go there and ride till she and her horse were ready to drop. The horse would come back lathered and blowing, and Katherine coated in dust and sweat, but both had lost the wild in the eye they'd have before the ride."

"Thankee."

"For what?" The senator gave him a surprised look.

"For sharing that with me." He didn't know why he should care, but he did. Somehow, he felt better knowing it. Without horses, Katherine would have withered and died. Reuben climbed into the saddle. The senator followed suit and they turned their mounts toward home.

"Reuben."

"Yeah?" His raspy voice gruff as he tried to ignore the fire shooting through ripped flesh, torn muscles and sensitive nerves.

"You took a bullet for me. I won't forget it."

CHAPTER 10

"Why is it you have to step in front of every dadblamed bullet that comes flying through the air? I've never known anyone who's taken as many as you have and haven't been plugged straight through the heart." Soggy fussed as he cleaned Reuben's wound, rinsing out the cloth he used in a basin filled with pinkish-colored water.

Reuben wisely said nothing.

Hawk's gaze tracked the room.

The senator watched the proceedings, his fingers thrumming against his thighs.

Her features pasty white, Sage chewed on her lower lip. Her gaze traveling back and forth between the big bulky rancher sitting in a hard-backed chair in the kitchen and the tall, lanky man that was her father, who stopped thrumming and began to pace.

"Senator, stop your pacing and pour us all a whiskey," Soggy snapped, as he finished dabbing at the front of the wound and went to work where it exited.

The senator gave a helpless look around as if trying to figure out where they hid the whiskey.

"I'll get it, sir," Hawk volunteered, having been in

the kitchen enough to know where Soggy kept the bottle.

"I'll get the glasses," Sage said, as if happy to have something to do. She hustled to the cabinet.

The wall cabinets where the dishes were kept were painted white and had no doors, except for the cabinet in the corner where the bottle and other sundry items were stored.

Hawk's eyebrows rose as Sage thumped down four glasses.

She looked him in the eye and notched her chin. He shrugged and poured a dollop in each glass. She tossed hers down and immediately began to cough. And cough. And cough. She gasped for breath, her face red. He patted her on the back.

When she'd caught her breath, she whispered, "Why do you men drink this nasty tasting stuff?" Then blinked. "It does warm the belly, doesn't it?"

Reuben snorted.

Soggy did too. "Headstrong. But then what can you expect given your lineage."

A tension-fraught quiet fell over the room. All eyes turned his way. Soggy looked like he was trying to swallow his tongue and busied himself with Reuben's wound.

He picked up the whiskey and poured a healthy amount on the hole in Reuben's arm.

"Dammit, Soggy," Reuben sputtered. His breath whistling through his teeth.

"What did you mean about my lineage, Soggy?"

Sage's question hung in the air.

Color washed through the older man's face, darkening wrinkles and accentuating white whiskers.

"Your mother was the most headstrong filly I knew." He jerked up his head, his tone pugnacious.

Her glance traveled from him to Reuben, whose jaw was locked, his eyes staring out the east window where the sun was trying to shine. Soggy wound a clean white cloth around Reuben's upper left arm. The muscles in Reuben's forearm dancing as he clenched and unclenched his fist.

The senator's face dead white.

"And my father?"

She threw a smiling look at her father, a smile that didn't reach her eyes.

"One of the most honorable men I know," Soggy answered sincerely.

"That must be some potent whiskey," Hawk muttered and took a sip.

"What did you say?" Sage whipped in his direction, her chestnut hair flaring then settling.

"Nothing."

She didn't push it and Hawk gave a mental swipe to his brow then realized she was just taking a different tack.

"So, who was this man shooting at?"

"Hard to say," Reuben rolled his sleeve down over his freshly bandaged arm, flexed his fingers and turned a wince into a grimace.

"It was you who got shot, which would indicate if he was any kind of shooter at all, you were the target."

"I've made enemies," was all he said.

Hawk glanced from Reuben to the senator. Something wasn't adding up. Reuben, a man who didn't hesitate to say what was on his mind, was being evasive and the senator looked like he'd swallowed a rock.

The senator downed his whiskey and said into the silence, "He got shot because he knocked me off my horse and took the bullet meant for me."

"I thought you didn't want her to worry," Reuben said dryly.

"Well now, she'd be worrying about one of us regardless."

"She'd be worried about you. She hasn't known me long enough to expend any worry in my direction." His face expressionless, Reuben picked up his glass and drained it.

"Is this the first time this has happened?" she asked her father through tight lips.

He didn't answer which was answer enough.

"How dare you." Sage drew herself up, color rising and falling in her face, her heart beating strong against her cornflower-blue shirt. She pointed her index finger at the senator. "How dare you try to keep this from me."

"Now, honey—" He rose to his feet

"And how dare you try to protect me from this or think I wouldn't care." Her voice broke, as she skewered Reuben with a glare.

Reuben gave her an astonished look. His jaw dropped and his eyebrows rose. Hawk chewed on a grin to see his tough-as-leather boss at a loss for words.

"Did you know about this?" She whirled on Hawk.

"No, ma'am." He tossed his hands in the air in an I-didn't-know-a-thing gesture.

"Soggy?"

"First I've heard about it."

"How long have you been getting threats?" She looked directly at her father, her arms crossed, her toe tapping and her eyes sparking.

"Darlin, I've been getting threats ever since I took office. You know that."

"Backed up by bullets," she ground out.

He sighed in defeat.

"The vitriolic notes starting coming about two months ago. Last month someone tried to knife me."

"How did you keep that, not only from me, but out of the papers?"

He laughed. "That surprised me too. It happened in a dark alley and no one was the wiser."

"You fought him off? Alone?" The surprise in her voice spoke volumes. All the men winced in comradery of threatened masculinity.

"I'm not completely helpless you know," the senator responded crisply.

"I know, Daddy. I know. Is that when you said you'd pulled a muscle in your side?"

"Yeah."

"So he stuck you."

"Yeah, then I got the knife and he got away."

"Any chance it's the same hombre?" Reuben asked.

"Same height. Same build. But the fellow wore a

mask. I just don't know." He gave a helpless shrug. "And even if he hadn't worn a mask, that fellow from the top of the canyon didn't have much of a face left to recognize."

"So, someone might still be after you." She turned to the window and stared out of it, but Hawk doubted if she was seeing either the coy sun flirting with a fluffy gray and white cloud or the two bay horses in the corral.

"Honestly, I just don't know. All I can do is business as usual."

The senator came up to her and put his arms around her.

She put her head on his shoulder.

"Even though I'll miss you like crazy, I'm glad you're here. Here. Where Reuben will keep you safe."

"You think I'm afraid?" She jerked away from him. Those magnificent eyes blazing.

"I could only wish." He heaved a heartfelt sigh. "My darling Sage, it will be one less thing for me to worry about." His gaze slid over Hawk. He didn't say anything but the message was clear. He wasn't completely easy about it, regardless of his words.

Hawk met the senator's gaze with equanimity and wondered yet again what he was doing here instead of moving on to another town, maybe in Mexico, swilling tequila and flirting with pretty senoritas. His gaze slid of its own accord to Sage.

Soggy, the senator and Reuben all glared at him. A message of warning on all their faces. The only one he worried about was Reuben's. The man might be twice his age but he was tough as nails. Reuben drilled him for a moment longer then nodded.

"I'll make sure she's unharmed. In any way." Reuben's meaning clear.

Seemed unfair to Hawk. If anyone walked away from this situation with a mangled heart, he had a feeling it would be he. The senator wasn't about to let his only daughter marry a hired gun.

He straightened. A chill ran down his spine. Marry? Where had that come from? Just because the young lady was no one to be trifled with didn't mean he needed to marry her.

He shuddered.

"Ghost walk on your grave?" Reuben asked.

The man didn't miss a thing.

"Something like that."

The senator turned to Reuben.

"I appreciate your hospitality. Now that I know Sage is alright, I'll head back to St. Louie then on to the capital."

"Daddy, you just got here."

"When things calm down a bit, I'll be back." He gave her a reassuring smile.

"Things never calm down."

"We'll make sure they do. Now, I'm going to ride back to town and take the next stage out."

"I'll ride with you."

"Sage, I'd prefer we say our goodbyes here. If someone is after me, I'm hoping they haven't made the connection that I came to see you."

"I'll ride with you," Reuben said then added before

Sage could protest, "Did you get your shooting lesson in?"

"Couldn't. It was pea soup out there," Hawk said.

"I suggest you do that now."

"Go, Sage." The senator kissed her on the forehead.

She bit her lips. It was obvious she wanted to protest. Finally, she said, "You take care of yourself, Daddy."

"I will and I'll let you know when it's safe to come home."

"No one has made any attempt to hurt me," she protested.

"And let's keep it that way. I know Reuben will make it a priority." He threw Reuben a brief look. Reuben returned it. His eyes dark and his lips in a straight line. He didn't bother to nod. There was no need.

CHAPTER 11

Clip-clop-clip-clop. Clip-clop-clip-clop.

The horses loped easily across the prairie. The Appaloosa's legs churning up tufts of grass and dirt, his tail swishing. The senator pushed the bay mare he was riding to keep up. She tossed her head, snorted then obliged.

As Mobeetie came into view, they reined the horses to a trot.

"Looks like you made it just in time." Reuben pointed to the end of the street where a dusty stage stood waiting. A young boy in worn canvas pants and a tan shirt led away the four horses pulling the coach, their sides liberally flecked with foam.

"I need to stop at the boarding house and grab my carpetbag. I had put a change of clothes in my satchel before I came to the ranch but my bag has my essentials including a couple of bills I'm working on."

"You go hold the stage. I'll get your bag."

The senator started to dig in his pocket for his wallet.

"Go. We can settle up later."

The senator nodded, thumped the bay with his heels and trotted down the street.

Reuben pulled in and tied his horse to a hitching post, then strode into the lobby of the boarding house.

Flowered yellow wallpaper lined the walls and a honey-colored wood counter stood in the center of the lobby, Mz. Krause behind it.

A young man in a black suit and a bowler hat, with blonde curls sticking out from under it, stood in front of it.

"Can you tell me if the senator is staying here?"

Reuben caught her eye and gave a small shake of his head. The man had reporter written all over him.

"And would you be referring to Senator Maxey, sir? 'Cause I can tell you we don't see him all that much in Mobeetie." She looked over the young man's shoulder and gave Reuben a wink.

"And who might that be?" the young man asked.

"Why our beloved Texas senator, sir. Who else would you be asking about?"

"Senator Baylor." He whipped the register, that she had a hand laid on, toward him and pointed in triumphant. "Not only the Senator but his daughter as well. Although, it appears she's already checked out."

Reuben's heels sunk into burgundy carpeting as he stepped forward.

"You got a problem here, Agatha?"

"I don't know yet. I'm waiting to hear why this young man is interested in my boarders."

"I'd like to know that too." Reuben stepped into the young man's space. The young man tried to take a step back and ran smackdab into the counter.

"I'm a reporter for the *Times,* out of St. Louie." He held out his hand. Reuben took it in a grip that made the young man wince, but he gamely shook it.

When Reuben released it, the reporter whipped out a small, worn notebook and a pencil from his vest pocket, licked the pencil tip then held it to the notebook.

"And you are?"

"Reuben Hayes."

"That's h-a-y-e-s?" He licked the pencil again.

"And just why would you want to know?" Reuben wasn't known for his patience and what little he had was quickly being used up.

"Why, I wanted to know if you'd seen Senator Baylor about town."

"I definitely haven't seen him about town." He looked around the lobby then pointed into the sitting room where a man's head was hidden behind a newspaper. The only thing visible: long, thin fingers and long legs encased in pinstriped black pants, crossed, wearing glossy black ankle boots.

The young reporter hurried over to the gentleman hiding behind the newspaper, giving it an occasional shake.

"I need your boarder's carpetbag. I'll settle up his bill when young Mark Twain ain't around."

She opened a drawer on the desk and slid him a key.

"Second floor. First door on the left."

"Much obliged, Agatha."

"He out at your ranch with the daughter?"

"Getting ready to head back to St. Louie on the next stage." He gave her a quick grin, tossed the key in the air, caught it and trotted up the stairs, his heels clicking as the disgruntled young man headed back.

"Try the saloon," he called from the top of the stairs.

The young man nodded and hurried out.

Reuben unlocked the door, grabbed a plain olive-green carpetbag, took a quick look around for incidentals and went clomping down the stairs. He stopped by the desk and pulled out his wallet.

"How much?"

"Three dollars."

He tossed down a couple of two-dollar notes and headed for the door.

"Wait, Reuben. You've got change coming."

He waved a hand over his head and kept going, hitting the sidewalk just as the stage was going by.

"Sylvester, wait," he bellowed.

A wiry little man with a huge black beard sawed on the reins.

"What you want, Reuben? I've got a schedule to keep."

He tossed the carpetbag through the open window of the stage. The senator caught it and nodded.

"Drive on, Sylvester."

Sylvester nodded and slapped the reins. The stage jerked forward and the fresh horses trotted out of town.

Disgruntled, the reporter came striding out of the Red Horse Saloon. He saw Reuben and headed toward him.

"He wasn't there."

Reuben gave one last look at the stage disappearing, dust rising beneath its wheels then settling back to the ground, and in high good humor, gave the reporter a whack on the back that nearly had his nose meeting the street.

"There's a lot more saloons in town to try." He settled his gun on his hip, strode to his horse and trotted out of town.

CHAPTER 12

Bang.

The end of a freshly budded oak branch drifted on the wind in a slow dance, making its graceful journey to the ground.

Sage turned toward Hawk with a wide smile, waiting for approval.

"Is that the limb you were aiming at?"

Her forehead corrugated in a frown and her bottom lip stuck out. He had the strongest desire to run a thumb along the protruding member then thought about shooting his hand off to keep it from going where it didn't belong, reminding himself Reuben would have no problem shooting it off for him.

"Yes." The frown deepened.

"Fine job." He flashed her a smile that usually had young ladies falling in with anything he suggested. Then again there was nothing usual about this particular young woman.

"Humph." She holstered her pistol with a little more force than necessary, strode to her horse and climbed on.

He looked at her for a long moment then shrugged

and vaulted lightly onto his pinto.

Ignoring him, she clucked to her horse and headed north.

"Hey, the ranch is back that way." He tapped the pinto and caught up with her.

"Feel free to go back then."

"And if I do, how much longer do you think you'll be allowed to ride out or not be sent packing for that matter?"

"Point taken." Her eyes flashed.

Hawk noticed, with amusement, that she didn't seem regretful or shamed, just displeased with the situation. He doubted if she was used to depending on any man for anything.

"So where are we going?"

"To the stream where I saw Blue."

"You and Reuben do seem enamored of that wild stallion."

"All you've got to do is look at him to know he's something special. His spirit, his courage. His pride." Her haughtiness vanished as her enthusiasm for the horse took over.

"What makes you think he'll be there?"

"If not, he'll come." Her voice rang with confidence, making him believe her in spite of his natural skepticism.

"But how do you know?"

She put her hand on her heart and answered simply, "I know in here."

"So, you think you have a connection?" he asked, intrigued.

"I do with him. I'm not so sure he does with me." She laughed. Easy. Confident.

"I guess we'll see." He clucked to his horse. The pinto broke from a trot to an easy lope. The chestnut followed suit. The scent of fresh and green rose from fleshy blades of grass and teased his senses as the wind blew away any tension between them.

They reined in atop the hill overlooking the meandering creek where Sage had spied Blue and his herd. Hawk leaned on the saddle horn and gazed into the empty valley then glanced at Sage and raised his eyebrows.

"He'll come." Her voice brimmed with confidence. She breathed deep of the fresh air then relaxed in the saddle.

Moments later a horse trumpeted and hooves thundered into the valley.

Hawk's mouth dropped and he gave her a disbelieving look.

She laughed. The sound not carrying to the milling horses as they spilled out and ranged along the stream to lap up the clear, rippling liquid. After the mares drank their fill and spread out to graze, a lone black mare, heavily pregnant, came limping in. Putting as little weight on her front left leg as possible. She wove between the other mares till she made her way to the stream and drank thirstily then waded into it to soak her bum leg. The water stopped short of her upper leg where a nasty jagged tear was visible, bloody skin flapping.

Sage made a sound of distress in her throat and

her face drained of color. "She can't possibly survive out here."

"Kindest thing would be to shoot her and put her out of her misery."

"Don't even think about it," she snapped through thin lips.

"It would be better than letting that mare wither away and die in pain," Hawk insisted.

"She won't." Sage's lips were firm, her voice decisive. Determination rode her features.

"And how do you figure that?"

"We're taking her back with us."

He digested this. He couldn't, wouldn't let Sage loose in the midst of a band of wild horses. He glanced over at her proud profile. Shooting that horse would break her heart. Though, still and all, it might come down to her heart or his hide when Reuben was factored into the equation.

He reached for his gun.

"Hawk." She said nothing more, but her expressive face said everything.

He considered his options, gave a sigh and capitulated. "What do you want me to do?"

When Sage turned a bright, grateful smile on him, he decided whatever the outcome, it was worth it.

"Just saunter on down there. The stallion will round up his mares and take off. Our mare will limp after him. When she does, rope her," Sage said, gathering her reins.

At that moment, the wind shifted lifting Sage's hair and blowing their scent to the stallion. He reared on steely gray hooves and hit the ground with a thud. Trumpeting out a command, he nipped at his mares to get them moving. Dust flew as they took off at a hard gallop.

Water splashed and rose in sparkling arcs as the hurt mare hobbled out of the water, whinnying her distress.

The stallion wheeled and came loping back to the injured mare, neighing encouragement.

Hawk lifted his hat then shoved it back on his head. He knew this wasn't going to be easy.

"Heeya." Hawk leaned forward in the saddle and sent his horse galloping toward the stallion. The pinto stumbled halfway down, throwing Hawk forward against the saddle pommel. The chestnut, who'd been directly behind, swerved around his horse and went racing down the rise.

He lifted the pinto with his knees and reins. His mount righted itself and tore down the hill.

Sage threw a quick look over her shoulder. Reassured that he was alright, she turned her attention to Blue and the injured mare.

The stallion trotted back and forth between the mare and the two approaching riders, tossing his mane, trumpeting his defiance.

Hawk snagged his lariat as the distance between them shortened and began to whirl it in the air, yipping, not sure what he'd do if that cussed horse didn't back down.

A mare screamed from the herd. Blue tossed his head, gave a militant bugle and took off in a cloud of dust. Hawk shot by Sage, twirled the lariat and let it fly.

It hovered above the mare. For one unsettling minute, Hawk thought he was going to miss, then it dropped and settled over the mare's head.

Before he could stop her, Sage was off her horse and running toward the mare.

The mare reared, her bad leg dangling in the air.

"Sage, get back," he yelled, his heart thumping, fearing she would catch a hoof in the temple.

Her step slowed. For a moment, he thought she was going to do as he'd commanded.

Instead, she stretched out her hand and, little by little, advanced on the hurt mare, her voice low, soothing.

Hawk leaped off his horse and strode forward, walking the rope, then stopping as the horse came down and stood trembling on her three good legs. His heart jumped to his throat as Sage reached out her hand and continued her slow but relentless approach. She stopped inches from the mare who'd backed as far away as the rope would allow and stood trembling violently.

Slowly, Sage reached in her pocket, pulled out a sugar lump and held out her hand again, still speaking quietly. Closer now, he could hear her. It was a crooning, almost a singing, that seemed to carry and blend with the wind. Words undistinguishable, just soft, reassuring sounds.

The mare's nose twitched as she smelled the sugar. She leaned her neck forward, without moving her body, then snapped it back, then tried again, and again drew it back. Finally, she took a step forward, nibbled the sugar cube then tossed her head.

"There now, that wasn't so bad was it," Sage crooned. The horse snorted. The trembling had lessened but not stopped. Then she rolled her eyes toward Hawk and reared again, her bad leg dangling, dried blood and pus coating it.

Sage ducked as the mare's good leg came a hairsbreadth from her head.

"Get on your horse," he snapped in a voice he'd never used with her before. A voice he seldom used period.

Her brows rolled together like thunder, but she obeyed. Turning on her heels and moving swiftly to her mount, she vaulted into the saddle.

The mare continued to whinny and fight.

A trumpet sounded in the distance.

Sage nudged her horse past him and rode next to the mare.

"Sage, get back."

This time she flat-out ignored him and began to croon to the mare again. Unbelievably, the mare quieted though the whites of her eyes were still visible.

"Let's get out of here." He turned his horse and nudged it forward. Sage stayed next to the mare. Either her proximity or her horse's seemed to calm the injured animal.

They trotted up the rise and headed for the ranch. The mare stumbling on three legs at the end of the rope.

The trumpeting of the stallion grew closer.

The mare whinnied in response.

Then they saw him, running straight at them.

"Crazy horse," he muttered, tightening the rope and drawing the mare closer.

"He's amazing," Sage breathed.

Hawk grunted and drew his gun.

"What are you doing?" Her eyes widened and her breasts heaved. Alarm writ on her features, as she pushed back a stray lock of hair that the wind whipped in her face.

Ignoring her, he fired the pistol in the air, causing the stallion to falter and the mare to swerve and stumble.

"With the stress she's under we'll be lucky if she doesn't go into labor before we get to the ranch."

"Tell that to your stallion."

"He won't follow us much farther. He won't endanger the entire herd for one mare, though it will gall him that he couldn't protect her."

"And how do you know what would gall that big brute?" Hawk glanced over his shoulder. Sure enough, the stallion had stopped. He rose on his hind legs, bugled a challenge then galloped away. Even from here, Hawk could see the clouds of dust those powerful hooves dug in the dirt. A measure of relief surged through him.

"What would you do if you were in his shoes?"

"I don't think like a horse and a horse don't think like me."

"You're right. More like a mule." She glowered at him.

"Pot calling kettle," he responded.

"Now you are calling me a mule?" A graceful eyebrow rose.

"If the horseshoe fits." He shook his head at the actions of the both of them. He hadn't indulged in such childish bickering since, well, since he was a child. He breathed a sigh of relief as the house and stable came into view.

As to be expected, the mare, who'd quieted with the desertion of the stallion, her head hanging in acceptance, took exception to entering the barn.

"Throw open that box stall in the back," Hawk said.

Sage bulleted into the barn and threw open the door. He got the mare to the stall, climbed off his horse and pulled the mare, now too exhausted to put up much of a fight, inside. He tied the rope wrapped around her neck to an iron hook by the front of the door. "Let's get her wound seen to then I'll untie her and we'll let her rest in peace."

She threw him a grateful look and raced through the barn, heading for the house. Sooner than he would have thought possible, she was back with Soggy in tow.

Dust motes danced in late afternoon sunlight as the two came through the stable door. Soggy carrying a wooden crate of medical supplies. Hawk's nose wrinkled at the smell of garlic and bacon grease along with the pungent scent of linseed.

With his bandy-legged gait, Soggy strode toward him, a worn towel with a hole in it tied around his waist. Sage trotted beside the cook carrying a bucket that Hawk could hear water sloshing in.

Soggy stopped in front of the stall and squinted at the mare. Taking a hard look at the gash on her upper foreleg.

"This her?"

"Yup."

The attention caused the mare to move restlessly.

"You're going to have to hold her still while I work on her. I don't have no desire to be smashed up against the stall."

"I'll go in with you. I can help quiet her."

Soggy paused.

"No, ma'am. You aren't," Hawk said.

She notched her chin.

Hawk gave her look for look.

"Let her in." Reuben had come in unnoticed. Light on his feet for such a big man.

Hawk stared in disbelief. The blood rushed through his system then sunk to his feet before it rushed back again. "You can't be serious."

"Her mom had a way with horses. Sage does too."

Sage threw Reuben a blinding look of gratitude then let herself into the stall with Soggy behind her. The horse whinnied and began to lurch around the boxy wooden structure. She went to its head and talked in low soft tones and the mare quieted.

She threw a quick look at Reuben and her eyes widened. He had moved to the front of the stall and stood with his arms crossed. His six-shooter in his right hand.

"What's that for?" She kept the calm in her voice and her body relaxed for the horse's benefit but her eyes held alarm.

"Just in case that hoss proves me wrong."

"You wouldn't shoot her." Her voice still calm, panic built in her eyes.

"Only if you were in danger."

"Well, don't worry about me," Soggy grumbled, causing Hawk to bite back a smile.

"I'll never forgive you if you hurt this horse," she said, her voice still calm and low.

"I know. Now get to it and get out of there."

Soggy took a clean rag and dipped it in the bowl of water then wrung it out. As he slapped it on the horse's leg, the mare moved restively.

"Here let me."

Soggy looked at Reuben.

He gave a clipped nod and Soggy stepped aside. Before anyone could object, Sage balanced the box on top of the stall post, moved into Soggy's space and began to clean the wound, talking to the mare.

Nerves quivered and danced under the mare's skin. She threw her head up and down a couple of times, but stayed quiet under Sage's gentle touch while she cleaned the wound. While she sewed up the flapping skin. While she plastered the healing paste Soggy had made.

Hawk watched in disbelief, never having seen anything like it.

When Sage was safely out of the stall, he took the rope from the mare's head then turned to Sage. Their companions, and everything around them, faded into the distance.

"That was the most amazing thing I've ever seen." With no thought or hesitation, he drew her into his arms and kissed her, and was rocked right down to his toes. He heard a buzzing in his ears. A buzzing that slowly morphed into a clearing of the throat. The throat was cleared again.

With great difficulty he set Sage away from him. Her expression as dazed as he knew his was. He looked at her for a long, long moment then raised his head and looked directly into the piercing gray eyes of Reuben Hayes.

"I'm dead." He said it with resignation and no hope.

"What?" Sage mumbled. Then as her surroundings came back into focus, looked around and gasped.

"Missy, go get the mare some oats."

"But—"

"Now." Reuben didn't raise his voice, but there was just something about the tone and the expression on his face that brooked no argument. Or maybe Sage was still as off kilter from the kiss as he was. Whatever the reason, to everyone's surprise, she left without another word, leaving the scent of verbena and horse in her wake.

Hawk straightened his shoulders, his expression resigned. He didn't even think about drawing his gun.

Whatever retribution Reuben chose to visit on him, he'd earned. What had he been thinking?

He hadn't, he admitted to himself ruefully. It seemed whatever common sense—not to mention self-preservation—he possessed, flew right out the window whenever he was around Sage.

Well, whatever Reuben intended to do, he'd best be doing it before he, Hawk, turned tail and ran, something he'd never done in his life.

"So, what's it going to be? Are you planning on pistol whipping me or stringing me up?" He straightened. It would have been a right fine display of courage if his voice hadn't cracked at the end.

Reuben looked at him. Saying nothing.

Hawk barely stopped himself from shuffling his feet.

Finally, Reuben spoke. "Ten years ago, hell five, I would have done both. But I've mellowed in my old age."

Soggy gave an inelegant snort that Reuben ignored.

"What are your intentions regarding Sage?"

Hawk blinked. His jaw dropped and his mouth dried. He started coughing. Soggy reached over and gave him a hearty whack on the back that nearly sent him sprawling.

"Sir, I have no intentions, good, bad or otherwise."

"Well, boy, just this once I'm going to give you a pass, but if I catch you kissing her again without having put a ring on her finger, we're going to have that discussion you mentioned and I can guarantee you that pretty face of yours ain't a'gonna be pretty any longer." He turned on his heel and headed for the house, Soggy beside him.

Hawk longed to ask him why he should care if Sage wasn't his daughter, then decided he had no wish to have his face rearranged and kept his lips clamped shut.

CHAPTER 13

"Boy's got it bad," Soggy observed as they trudged to the house.

"Yeah," Reuben responded, a fine powdering of dirt spurting underfoot and coating his worn boots as they passed the corral. "He just hasn't figured it out yet."

"Kinda surprised you didn't pistol whip him or shoot him."

"I'm getting soft in my old age."

Soggy snorted.

As they reached the porch, Reuben paused, his boot on the step, his hand shading his eyes, watching dust kicked up in the distance. "Rider coming."

They waited

The rider galloped under the HAYES RANCH sign and reined in at the porch.

"Can I help you, mister?" Reuben's hand rested on his gun.

"Looking for Hawk. Heard he's here." The cowboy was middle-aged, with a dark mustache and straggly beard.

"What would you be wanting him for?"

"Now, mister, I don't see how's that is any of your

business."

"You're on my property. So is he. That makes it my business." Reuben straightened. His eyes bore into the cowboy.

The cowboy's eyes narrowed. His hand inched to his gun.

Like lightning, Reuben's was out of his holster. The hammer clicked.

The rider shot his hands in the air.

"Well?" Reuben asked, his Peacemaker aimed at the man's heart.

The man spit a wad of tobacco on the ground, his hands still in the air. "Got a job offer for him. Appears the boss is offering it to the wrong man."

"He's in the barn."

"Okay if I lower my hands now?"

Reuben gave him a clipped nod.

The cowboy lowered his hands, reined his horse, and headed for the barn.

"Think he'll take it?" Soggy asked.

"We'll soon be finding out." Reuben climbed the porch steps and leaned a hip on the railing.

"Yup, we will. You think he'll stay?"

"Nope. He's running."

"That's the way I see it too." Soggy's expression glum. "Sure am glad we're too old to be dealing with any of that nonsense and can make decisions with what sits between our ears instead of our nether regions."

"Yeah."

"Now, who in tarnation is that?"

Reuben, whose gaze had been fastened on the barn, turned his attention to the dirt lane just as a buckskin came barreling toward them. He squinted at the rider wearing a suit and bowler. "It's young Dekker. Jinks Dekker."

"From the telegraph office?"

"Yup."

"You'd think it was Sunday-Go-To-Meetin', and that this was the church, as many riders as we're getting," Soggy said.

"Yeah." Reuben holstered his gun.

Dekker hauled his mount in at the base of the porch. The horse blowing, nostrils red and flaring, flanks flecked with foam.

"Jenks, you got a reason for pushing that horse so hard?" Reuben stuck his hands in his back pockets, rocked on his heels and hoped to hell it wasn't bad news.

"That's for you to decide, sir." Jenks pulled a telegram out of his pocket, bent in the saddle and handed it to Reuben.

"Thankee."

Reuben tossed him a couple of coins.

"You're most welcome, sir, and thank you." He tipped his bowler, turned his horse around and trotted out of the yard at a more decorous pace. The stranger who'd come to see Hawk, came out of the barn, touched heels to flanks and went galloping past Jenks, leaving a trail of dust in his wake.

Reuben fumbled in a vest pocket, pulled out his specs and read. His lips tightened, right along with his heart. So tight, he could swear all the blood drained from it.

"Well?" Soggy demanded belligerently.

Silently, Reuben passed him the telegram.

"Damn," Soggy said after reading.

"Yeah."

Hawk came striding out of the barn.

"What are you going to do?" Soggy asked.

"Whatever I have to."

Hawk stopped in front of them, a determined expression on his face.

"I've been offered another job."

"And?"

"If you're agreeable, I thought I'd take it."

"You signed on for a month. I'm holding you to it."

"Why? Under the circumstances, I thought you'd be pleased to see the last of me."

Reuben looked at Soggy and nodded. Silently, Soggy passed the telegram to Hawk.

Hawk scanned it. All color drained from his face. The paper crackled as he clenched it in his fist.

"I'll stay as long as you need me."

CHAPTER 14

If the bill passes, that pretty little girl of yours is dead.

There was more, of course, but those were the words seared on Hawk's brain. From the gist of the telegram, the senator had arrived home and found the note slid under his door.

"What's this about?" He followed Reuben and Soggy into the kitchen as Reuben made a beeline for the dented, granite coffee pot.

"Just what it says. Apparently, the senator is still getting death threats about a bill he's trying to pass."

"And since those aren't working, they're threatening his daughter?"

"Appears so."

"Then he needs to put it on the backburner."

"If Sage is being threatened, I'm sure that's what he'll do." Reuben heaved a sigh.

"The bill. It's an important one?"

"It's important," Reuben said, his voice a notch gruffer than usual. He nudged a jar of peaches aside and leaned against the wood counter, a spattering of flour adhering to the arms of his faded red shirt.

"Does anyone besides the senator know she's here?"

"There was a young reporter nosing around. Don't know if he figured it out or not. I think I'll go pay him a visit." He ground his teeth when he spoke and clenched his fists.

"I'll go with you."

"You stay here."

Anger hot and bright shot through him, but before he could protest, Reuben said, "From here on out, one of us is with her at all times."

Chagrin replaced the mad and he nodded.

"Don't count me out." Soggy gave a pugnacious raise of his chin and reached for the old Winchester in the corner of the kitchen.

"That's one thing, I'd never do. If the first line falls, no one will be getting through you and Betsy." Reuben nodded toward the rifle.

"As long as you know it." Soggy gave a sharp jerk of his chin and, with the worn towel he wore around his waist, rubbed at a nonexistent piece of dust on the barrel before he stuck the rifle back in the corner of the kitchen.

"I do." Reuben poured himself a cup of coffee, wincing a little as he picked up the pot with his bum arm.

"I don't suppose there's any point in telling you I could have poured that for you," Soggy fussed.

"I ain't exactly handicapped, Soggy."

Hawk bit down on a grin. Soggy was like a hen with one chick where his tough-as-rawhide boss was concerned.

"Where is Sage anyhow?" Reuben leaned back

against the counter and sipped his coffee.

"Out in the barn fussing over the mare."

"Then you better hie out there yourself. And I don't think there's any need to mention this to her."

"She might be on her guard more if she knew," Hawk responded, chewing on the command. Not sure he agreed with it.

"She might. But she's fretting enough about her pa. There's no point in us putting more on her plate."

"Your call." Though he didn't agree with it. It made him edgy. Not his decision, he reminded himself.

"Yeah, it is." Reuben thumped his cup down on the counter, causing the liquid to shoot in the air. But even the coffee, it seemed, wouldn't dare get Reuben pissed off and plopped with precision back in the cup.

"I'm heading in town." He tromped out of the house. The door slamming behind him.

"And I'm going to the barn."

"Good. Get out of the kitchen and let me get on with putting together vittles for supper. You'd think I didn't have anything better to do than stand around jawing all day with the two of you." He pulled a skillet out of the cabinet and slammed it on the stove with a bang.

Hawk grinned and headed out the door. He hit the porch as Reuben's big Appaloosa went galloping under the ranch sign, creaking as a stiff breeze caught it. He settled his hat more firmly on his head as the brisk air made a determined play for it.

As he strode into the barn, the sweet scent of hay and horse vied with the scent of rain the breeze blew his way. He trod down the wide dirt floor till he got to the last stall, ground in his heels and halted in the shadows.

She wasn't even aware of his presence, all of her focus on the horse as she talked to it in soft, unintelligible words, her hands softly stroking the mare's neck.

How would it feel to be the center of all that gentleness and love, he wondered?

And at that exact moment, if there had been any doubt before, there was no longer. He was in deep trouble.

He'd grown up a lonely child in a mission orphanage and headed out before he turned fifteen. He'd fallen in with an aging shootist who had taught him how to handle a gun and shortly after got himself killed. Now he lived by his wits and gun and relied on no one. People just disappointed.

It would bear keeping in mind before he got too attached to these folks. Reuben, tough but fair. Soggy, a bantam rooster with a heart of gold. And this beautiful woman, with the clear gray eyes, that seemed to see through all the barriers he'd thrown up to look into his soul. Someone who could shred his heart until it lay bleeding and in pieces at her feet. He should hightail it out today. This very minute. But he couldn't. Not till he knew she was safe.

He let out a gusty sigh. Focused on the mare, she didn't hear him. But the horse did. The mare snorted, tossed her head and moved to the back of the stall.

Distracted, Sage looked around. "She's in labor."

Sure enough a spasm passed across the big black belly and the mare grunted.

"Looks that way." At Sage's troubled expression, he added, "Don't worry, mares foal all the time."

She peered at him in disgust and gave a snort that would have done the horse proud. "Did you hear that, Darling? Mares do it all the time. Isn't that just like a man?"

"What can I do to help?" Hawk was nothing, if not a quick learner.

She threw him a grateful look.

His chest swelled before he gave himself a mental shake at his own gullibility. Next thing he knew, she'd be putting a bit in his mouth and leading him around the paddock.

"I've never been around a mare foaling before. I don't know what to do for her."

"You're doing exactly what she needs. You're giving her comfort. The rest she'll manage on her own."

As if to mock his words, the wind picked up whistling around the barn and rain began to pelt the wood-shingled roof. Thunder boomed and lightning struck nearby, causing the mare to wicker and nerves to quiver under her skin, transferring her unease to the stoic cowboy.

CHAPTER 15

Click clack.

Reuben clomped along Main Street, hot, tired and wet. A damp tumbleweed came blowing down the sidewalk and hit his black slicker before sliding to the ground. Rain fell steadily, dripping off the brim of his Stetson, doing nothing to cool the heat or thin the thick air.

As he pushed through the doors of the Red Horse Saloon, a drunken cowboy came reeling out.

"Watch where you're going, Grandpa," the cowboy who didn't look much younger than Reuben mumbled as he bounced off the solid wall of Reuben's chest and back into the saloon.

"Who you calling grandpa?"

"You old man."

Still running on raw nerves from the telegram, Reuben put his fists between the drunk's eyes. "I ain't your grandpa."

Lying flat on his back, the drunk reached clumsily for his gun.

"Well for—" Reuben waited till the gun left its holster before kicking it out of the hombre's hand.

"Who are you, old man?" The man howled,

nursing his hand.

"Reuben Hayes and I don't give a spit in hell who you are."

"Sorry, Mister Hayes. I didn't recognize you." The man's bloodshot eyes widened.

"Well, you're right about one thing, I must be getting old cause I ain't a'gonna kill ya." He stepped over the prone cowboy and headed for the bar.

"Joe."

"Reuben." The barkeep, a large, muscled man with a bald head, stood drying a shot glass.

"What can I get ya?"

"Beer." He pointed at the wooden keg.

Joe half turned then his eyes widened. "Look out."

The cowboy on the floor was raising his gun and pointing it at Reuben.

Lightning fast, Reuben whirled, drew his pistol and fired.

The hombre slumped to the floor, blood blooming on his chest.

"Damn." Reuben shook his head.

"He didn't leave you much choice," Joe said, as he slapped down a glass of foamy golden brew before nodding at two cowboys at the end of the bar and pointing at the body.

"No, he didn't." Reuben took a long gulp, felt his belly loosen and thumped the glass on the bar that glistened with shine. "Is that young reporter still around here?"

"Black suit, blond curls and wire specs?"

"Yeah, that would be him."

Joe pointed to a corner table where a young man sat on the edge of his seat, scribbling into a notebook, his gaze jumping back and forth between the body the cowboys were dragging out and his writing.

"Thanks."

Beer in hand, Reuben made his way to where the young cub reporter scribbled. The reporter looked up as Reuben's shadow fell across his table. He stared at Reuben his gaze unfocused before it sharpened and he frowned.

"You're the man that sent me on a wild goose chase."

"Maybe I thought you should be minding your own business." Reuben was fighting a strong urge to grab the young man by the throat and shake him till his teeth rattled, but just in case the reporter had nothing to do with what was happening to the Baylors, he'd hold onto his temper till he found out different.

"That's not in my job description."

"Maybe it should be." Reuben dropped down in the chair across from the reporter, took off his hat and shook the excess water on the floor.

"Have a seat," the reporter said dryly.

"I think I will."

"I'm Reuben Hayes." He held out his big, callused paw.

"George Story." The reporter took it.

"What's your real name not your byline." Reuben rolled his eyes.

"Believe it or not that is my real name." Behind his

glasses, his eyes twinkled.

"I don't."

"It was worth a try." He grinned. "George Schrijnemakers. It's Dutch and means cabinet maker."

Reuben grinned back, beginning to like the young reporter in spite of himself. "George Story. That's a right fine name."

George laughed and the remaining tension broke. "Reuben Hayes." George rubbed a clean-shaven chin. "I've heard of you."

Reuben waited.

"What can I do for you?" Then added, "Are you the one that drew down on that drunken cowboy? I had stepped out back when the action went down. I got back and a body was being dragged out." He shook his head. "Story of my life."

"What newspaper do you work for?"

"I'm an independent reporter." He shifted in his chair. Color came into his cheeks but he looked Reuben in the eye and lifted his chin when he spoke.

"In between jobs, huh?"

"Yeah."

"So why were you dogging Senator Baylor?"

"The Senator's news. If I could get one good story under my belt, I'm hoping the St. Louis Globe will take me on." Behind his glasses, George's blue eyes lit up.

"You from St. Louie?" Reuben leaned back in his chair and sipped his beer. His manner relaxed, no sign of the tight muscles and sparking nerves racing through his system.

"Yup." George took a sip of his sarsaparilla.

"Why didn't you go back home when the Senator did?"

"There's a reason for the Senator coming here and I'm going to find out what it is." He leaned across the table. The hot look of fanaticism in his eyes.

"Do you know anything about the attacks on the senator?"

"He's had several. He's a controversial figure. But there's more going on than that, isn't there? What can you tell me?" He grabbed his tablet and stuck his pencil in his mouth to wet it then held it poised. Waiting.

Reuben thrummed his fingers on the scarred table top and studied the young reporter. He'd learned to read men, but if he misread this one, he'd be making not just a mistake, but a fatal one. Finally, he said, "How would you like to do a bit of snooping for me?"

"And in return?"

"If you don't send the story in till I give you the okay, I'll make sure you get a scoop that should land you a job."

"About the senator?"

"About the senator."

"You've got yourself a deal." George held out his hand.

Reuben grasped it in his callused paw, feeling the jump of energy in the reporter's pulse and seeing the gleam of excitement in his eyes.

The first part of his plan now in place.

CHAPTER 16

A spear of lightning flashed through the night sky and landed a few yards away, causing the Appaloosa to snort and sidle as he trotted into the barn. Tufts of hay, interspersed with hard-packed earth, crumbled beneath the horse's large hooves, wafting an earthy aroma that smelled like heaven to Reuben.

Lantern light from a beam near the end of the barn lit his way. Gun in hand, Hawk whirled. Then shoved it back in his holster when he saw Reuben.

Indistinct murmuring came from the stall. Soggy. Sage. He couldn't make out the words but Sage's voice was laden with distress.

"What's going on?" He rode up and swung out of the saddle.

"Darling is having trouble delivering," Sage said through tight lips, her skin stretched tight across her cheekbones.

"Beg pardon?" For a moment, he stared at her blankly.

"She named the mare," Hawk said.

"Oh." He looked in the stall where the mare lay spasming.

Soggy wiped his hands in the straw and pushed to

his feet.

"What's happening?" Reben asked.

"One hoof is the only thing visible."

"How long?"

"Water broke an hour ago."

"Let's take a look."

"Bucket of water and a bar of soap on the floor there."

Reuben washed his hands then entered the stall. "Get her on her feet."

"Come on, Darling. That's a good girl. Get up now." While Sage coaxed and tugged on her bridle, Hawk moved into the stall and pushed on her wide flank to move her. Groaning and shaking her head, she pushed to her feet.

"Where's the rod wax?"

"On the post there." Soggy pointed to a round metal tin with a yellow lid and a paper label with *Vaseline Brand* lettered on it.

Reuben rolled up his sleeves and reached for the tin.

"What are you doing?" Sage asked.

"I got to see what's what."

She looked at his large callused hands.

"I'll do it." Her face took on a greenish hue.

"Are you sure about this?"

"Yes." She lifted her chin, an obstinate expression on her face that he'd seen reflected in his shaving mirror a thousand times.

"I'll walk you through it."

She took a deep breath and handed the halter to

Hawk.

"Wash your hands and grease up to the elbows."

She did as instructed.

"Now reach in and see if you can feel the other leg. If you can, straighten it out."

She bit her lips and put her hand inside the horse. The mare whickered in protest, her sides quivering.

"I'm sorry, Darling. I'm so sorry." Sage's voice caught, her expression distressed.

"Can you feel it?" Reuben asked.

"No." Her breathing came in short sharp pants.

"Don't faint on me, girl."

"No intention of it," she gasped out, looking even greener.

"Push the hoof back in and find that missing leg. Gently. Gently," he cautioned.

Her face scrunched, she reached in farther.

"I got it." Her eyes widened in relief.

"Okay. Now cup it in your hand so you don't tear the womb."

She bit her lips and leaned into the mare. "I've got it cupped."

"Good. Now bring it in and up, under the foal's neck. Gently."

She fumbled and the horse nickered in distress, trying to move away. Hawk held her fast. Grunting, Sage reached in further, her shoulders against the back of the mare's quivering hindquarters. Finally, she whished out a relieved, "Okay."

"Now if everything is lined up, pull on the legs."

Sage grunted and tugged.

Nothing happened.

She tugged again.

This time Darling gave a groan and pushed. Sage sat down in the straw abruptly. A squirming bloody sack in her lap.

"You did it, girl." Reuben grinned broadly, pride rushing through him and swelling his chest. He squatted down, broke the sac and cleaned out the colt's nostrils.

A clean rag sailed through the air. He caught it with his free hand and started rubbing down the foal. Another one followed and landed in Sage's vicinity. They both rubbed vigorously. The foal shook his head and tried to scramble out of Sage's lap. His spindly legs going in all directions. She gave a giddy laugh as Reuben put the foal on his feet and heaved Sage to hers.

He pulled a flask out of one of his vest pockets and handed it to her.

She grinned, took a short gulp, coughed, and handed it back. Reuben took a healthy swig and passed it to Hawk, who also took a gulp, handed it to Soggy, who took a swallow then handed it back to Reuben, who capped it and stuck the now empty bottle back in his pocket.

"You done a good job, girl."

"Darling deserves the credit." She grinned at him and continued cleaning the colt. The colt nudged Sage, then turned to his momma and began looking for the feed bag.

Hawk held up the lantern to get a better look at the

colt.

"Would you look at that," Reuben said, his hands in his back pants pockets.

Sage took a good look and gasped. "Oh my gosh, he looks just like his daddy."

At that moment lightning speared, lighting the sky outside the barn, and thunder boomed, shaking the ground, causing the colt to prance underneath his tired momma. The mare gave him a contented nuzzle.

"We've got to name him Thunder," Sage declared, hands on hips as if daring anyone to argue.

"Your colt, and mare for that matter. Name him what you will."

Her jaw dropped and her eyes widened then without thought she leaped into his arms. His heart stuttered, stopped, then jackhammered and his arms stole around her. She couldn't possibly love an old codger like him, it was just gratitude. Yet it sure felt like love. It felt like the affection a daughter would show her father. Regardless of what happened. Or of when she'd leave, he'd always have this one precious moment.

"I can't take them to St. Louis." She eased out of his arms and looked up at him.

"They'll be here whenever you come back to visit them."

"Thank you, Reuben." She gave him a blinding smile.

He swallowed past a humdinger of a frog in his throat. "I better see to my horse." He double-timed it out of the stall and led the Appaloosa toward the other end of the barn before he made a complete fool of himself. He started to speak. Nothing but a croak came out. He cleared his throat and called, "Better give that mare some extra oats, she's earned them."

While they fussed over the mare and colt, he saw to his horse. By the time everyone was ready to leave, the rain had stopped and the moon shone in a clear sky.

As they headed toward the house, he asked, "Would you like to see the old homestead tomorrow, get acquainted with your roots?" It wasn't in the hope of encouraging her to stay. Everyone needed to know where they came from. Sage was no exception. Or so he told himself. Then snorted. He always took and gave the truth straight up, no matter how hurtful. Truth was it was a good thing to know one's roots, but that was just sugar coating. He wanted her to stay pure and simple.

CHAPTER 17

The big Appaloosa and the smaller chestnut galloped across the plains. Showy orange butterfly weed popped up cheerful and bright against blades of emerald-green grass, still tinged with dew. The riders reined in on a hilltop, below them stood a ramshackle cabin gray with age. A barn falling down nearby.

"This is where she grew up?" Sage asked, leaning forward in the saddle. She wore a tan split-skirt that spread over the saddle and an orange blouse that matched the flowers growing beneath the horses' hooves. Apparently, a Monarch thought so too as it landed momentarily on her shoulder then flew away.

Sage, who normally would have been enchanted, barely noticed.

Her horse snorted and sidled, as if hands had tightened on the reins.

Memories bubbled over that Reuben would have as soon stay buried as he stared at the empty building. The windows, like the house's occupants, long gone.

"I'm surprised you don't knock it down and use it for grazing."

"I got a thousand acres of grazing land. I don't rightly need more."

"Why'd you buy it?"

He didn't like questions. Didn't like explaining himself and didn't make a habit of it. But it was Katherine's daughter doing the asking and she had a right to know.

"I thought someday Katherine would come home." He looked straight ahead while he spoke, pushing hard against the anger, hurt and loss that bubbled under the surface. She'd never be coming home now.

"Let's go." His voice came out harsher than intended.

He kicked the Appaloosa in the ribs and sent it thundering down the hill, reining in beside the falling down structure. As he threw a leg over the saddle, the chestnut came to a stiff-legged halt beside his mount. Throwing up dust that rose in a fine cloud before settling back on the ground.

Reuben stepped onto the porch. The board beneath his big-booted foot cracked.

"Stay behind me. This whole structure could come crashing down around our ears."

"Maybe I should go first. I weigh a few pounds less."

A laugh came rolling out of his throat as he glanced from his long, bulky body to her reedy figure. "A few."

As she started to walk in front of him, he stuck his arm out. "I'll go first."

"Eek." A squeak and scurry of a small furry critter running over her boot had her leaping back. "You win.

You go first."

He chuckled and stepped across the threshold. Dust rose beneath his boots. A pigeon nesting in the rafters gave a startled squawk and flew out the open, sagging window near the entryway. Putting his hands in his pockets, he rocked on his worn heels. From the entryway he could see into the kitchen and the living area. A rose-colored couch had turned to a dusty pink with droppings and the remains of nesting materials in it.

He strode into the kitchen and ran his hand over a pine table coated with fine, suety dirt. He rubbed a spot at the end of the table. The wobbly initials KW were on the very corner. Katherine had used her meat knife and carved the initials when she was ten years old. She'd gotten a scolding for it, but nothing more serious.

Quick footsteps sounded behind him. He moved aside and pointed at the initials.

A smile, so reminiscent of Katherine it took his breath away, spread over Sage's features. "She'd have had me sitting in a corner for a week if I'd carved my initials in the table."

"Your table is probably a bit fancier."

"Maybe, but I prefer this one."

She glanced over at a once white cabinet door, grayed by weather and hanging by one hinge. "Empty houses are sad, aren't they? It's like the soul of the inhabitants have moved on."

"Yeah." He turned on his heel and strode down the hallway. Sage's boots clicked briskly, sending up little puffs of dust as she followed.

They stopped in front of a bedroom. The door gone.

A ratty bedspread covered a double bed. The frame wooden and made by hand. A dirty green ceramic washbasin sat on a tall dresser with an empty nest in it.

"This must have been my grandparents' room."

"Yeah, it was."

A framed needlepoint of pink roses and lilies of the valley hung over the bed. The frame simple, painted pink and peeling. Sage took a step forward for a closer look and sneezed.

"Pretty," Sage commented.

"Your grandmother made it."

"It must have taken a long time."

It was a good-sized picture.

"She was always working on something." He could see her clearly in his mind. A gray-haired version of Katherine. Wireless specs on her nose, rocking back and forth in front of the river rock fireplace. Needle work in her roughened hands. Grinding-hard work had made her old before her time.

"Would you mind if I took the picture?"

"It's yours."

"Technically, it's yours."

"Anything you want in this house is yours."

"That's very generous."

"Not so much. It should belong to you."

"Regardless, thank you." She reached up and kissed his cheek.

Love rushed through him and rocked him to his toes. He cleared his throat. Once. Twice. And got himself under control.

"Want to see your mother's room?"

"Yes.

"Have you been through the house before?"

"After your mom left, I never set foot in it again."

"Not even after you bought it?"

"No."

Memories dogged his footsteps as they trod down a short hall and entered a room with tattered curtains at the open window. Pop-up gray clouds hovered over the sun, that had shone so bright earlier, and crowded a now dull sky. A thin mist coated the air and dropped to the ground.

Sage strode to the dresser and plucked something up. "Do you think this was my mom's?"

Hands in hip pockets, he turned from studying the weather and looked at the tarnished locket dangling from her fingers. The small heart a punch to the belly that would have taken him to his knees if he hadn't locked them.

"That's hers." His gravelly voice deep.

He'd given it to her the night before everything went to hell when she told him she was moving to St. Louie. That she didn't want to live in a rundown cabin in the middle of nowhere anymore and she wanted him to come with her.

He tightened his features into their usual impassive lines as she studied him. He was tough as old shoe leather except for Katherine and now her daughter.

"Are you my father?"

The question erupted from her throat and knocked him off his pins. His heart stuttered and his pulse slowed then exploded. His breath whished out of his lungs and his heart went from near stopped to galloping.

He looked her in the eye. It was one of his cardinal rules. Never apologize, never back down and always look whoever you're dealing with in the eye.

Silence built and pulsed between them. Her gaze just as direct as his.

"Your father is the man who raised you," he finally said, forcing himself not to shift on his feet.

"My daddy raised me and no one will ever take his place. Are you my father? The man who gave me life?"

The girl was smart as a whip but still, how did she know? He looked directly into gray eyes, same shape, same stormy color as his own and the same downward slash of the eyebrows when she was mad. How could she not know?

The silence built. He sucked in air and straightened his shoulders. "Yes."

"Did you know about me?" The question erupted, hoarse and harsh as she swallowed once, twice, three times then she too straightened her shoulders.

"If I had, nothing would have kept me away."

"Why didn't she tell you?"

He stared at the chain sliding through her fingers like tarnished gold, leaving thin strands of dust on her hands.

"We'd had a huge fight and both of us were stubborn as two mules."

"Why didn't you go after her?"

"If she'd wanted me, she knew where to find me."

"What did she say in her letter? Did she explain?"

"Haven't read it." He'd almost burned it then jerked the envelope back from the flames at the last moment. Had she hated him so much she'd kept his daughter from him for eighteen years?

The envelope, crumpled in his vest pocket, crinkled as if mocking him. Hurt and anger bubbled over.

"Why not read it? Don't you want answers?"

"She gave me a pretty straightforward answer when she left me. What else could she say?"

"That she loved you."

"You don't walk out on people you love. And now that you know who I am, where do we stand?"

"You tell me."

He took a heavy breath and looked her in the eye. "I want the eighteen years back that were stole from me, but since that's not possible, I want every spare minute you're willing to give me."

"The senator will always be my dad." She notched up her chin.

He rubbed his heart. It ached like the devil. A dull ache that promised to continue as it had every day since Katherine left him.

"He's your father in every way but blood. I understand you wanting to get back to him, I'll take you in town to catch the stage." He turned on his heel, heading for the door.

"Reuben."

He kept going, putting one foot blindly in front of the other. He needed the crisp whip of wind, the rustling of grass and his horse beneath his knees. This had been a bad idea.

"Reuben, wait." She caught up with him and stopped him by placing her hand on his arm.

"I didn't say I didn't want to stay. I care about you. I'd like to get to know you. I just want you to know I'll always love my dad. That will never change."

"Wouldn't expect you to feel any other way." He stared straight ahead, breaking his rule of always look the person you're jawing at in the eye.

"That doesn't mean there's not room in my heart for you too."

"You ready to go?" He gave a jerky nod and strode to his horse.

"It appears I am." She tried for a laugh, but it caught in her throat.

"Daddy knows?" She asked as she threw herself into the saddle.

"He knows."

"Has he always known?"

"Yeah."

"And he loved me anyway," she murmured.

"How could he not?" He lifted the Appaloosa into a trot, glancing around as he rode, his gaze traveling over everything and nothing.

She wheeled her horse till it trotted beside his.

"For a tough man, you can be charming."

His lungs no longer wheezed for oxygen and his heart no longer clenched tighter than a fist. "Don't mention that to the hands or I'll lose all standing," he joked.

She chortled.

A chuckle rumbled in his throat.

A jack rabbit darted across their path causing the chestnut to shy and for his focus to flip from his surroundings to his daughter. He reached for her horse's reins just as the shot rang out.

CHAPTER 18

With a noisy flutter of wings, blackbirds rose shrieking from a nearby tree.

Reuben grabbed his rifle, as he dove on Sage. Knocking her to the ground. Rolling so that he took the hit to earth that had no give. Curling around her, shielding her with his big body as another shot rang out.

Plastered over her, he fired in the direction the shot came from. The report from his Winchester loud in the quiet.

The sun inched from behind low-lying clouds, that darkened and roiled through the sky, glinting off a rifle barrel. Reuben aimed and fired in rapid succession. When his lever clicked on empty, he grabbed his six-gun and waited.

Silence.

He shifted and Sage grunted.

"Are you alright?" he asked, his gaze never shifting from the outcropping at the top of the hill where the shots had come from.

She didn't answer.

He moved his hand that lay on a bare spot in the grass. It came away wet and sticky.

"Are you hit? Where at?" His heart leaped to his throat and his mouth went dry. Still shielding her, he lifted his body. His gaze darting between her and the horizon.

Before she could answer, he ran his hand up and down her right side, balancing on his knees and one hand.

"Shoulder," she gasped out.

Her breath caught and he could hear her teeth grind as his fingers probed her right shoulder.

With an eye on the hilltop, he dug in his vest and pulled out his five-inch Texas Toothpick and opened it. Less worried about a bullet to the heart than seeing to Sage. He slit her shirt at the shoulder and cut off her sleeve, exposing a plain white chemise top, wth an inch-wide, shoulder strap stained red with blood.

He gave the ledge one more sweeping glance, then turned his attention back to his daughter.

"I could sure use a canteen about now," he muttered.

"Horses gone?" Her voice held a raspy quality that had his pulse jumping. Agitation coated his system.

"Yeah," he dabbed cautiously at the wound seeping blood a whole lot quicker than he liked. He wiped it away and breathed a sigh of relief. "Probably hurts like hell, but it's just a graze."

"You're right on the hurts like hell," she said between clenched teeth. The skin drawn taut across her bones had turned an unhealthy shade of yellow.

"Good thing you're tough like your mom." He cut the second sleeve from her other arm and made a dressing out of it, then cut one of his own sleeves off and tied it on her shoulder.

"Good thing I'm tough like you."

"Yeah." The icy fear clutching him loosened a bit as his leathery old heart warmed.

"There. That should hold you till we get home."

"And how do you propose we do that," she ground out, her teeth clenched.

The horses had galloped away.

"Let me worry about that. Right now, I have to see if our shooter is still up there." He jerked his head in the direction of the ledge.

"Reuben."

"Yeah?"

"Be careful."

"Count on it."

Bending low, he bulleted toward a wide oak a few yards away, expecting to hear the whine of a bullet any moment. His chest heaving, he paused behind the tree then, still bent over, raced toward a small boulder. When no shots were fired, he began to feel more confident and started zig-zagging up the hill.

Gun drawn, he reached the top and looked around.

The shooter was gone. In the distance, he saw a small puff of dirt heading toward Mobeetie. He scanned the ground. Hoof prints that had crushed small tufts of grass, and pushed down earth, were headed in the same direction.

Sage was safe for now.

He bulleted down the hill toward his daughter.

She lay still, her face white, her eyes closed.

"Sage."

"You came back." She opened them and gave him a strained smile.

"'Course I did."

He put his fingers between his lips and whistled, a shrill, carrying sound. A neigh sounded in the distance and the Appaloosa came galloping back. The chestnut long gone. No doubt heading for home.

Scooping up Sage, he sat her in the saddle, then jumped up behind her.

"How did you do that?" she marveled.

"We know each other." He clucked to the big stallion and touched boots to flanks. The horse broke into a trot and Reuben lifted it into a smooth lope. They'd covered about a mile when they saw the chestnut leisurely cropping grass, its flax-colored tail swishing at imaginary flies.

He rode up beside the mare grabbed the reins, tied them to the saddle pommel and continued on. By the time they arrived home, Sage was barely conscious.

As he reined the horses in, Hawk came charging out.

"What happened?" Without a by-your-leave Hawk grabbed her out of Reuben's arms.

"Ambushed," Reuben answered as Hawk carried her into the kitchen. His face as white as Sage's was yellow.

George Story rose from the table where he'd been sipping coffee.

Soggy took one look and began gathering supplies then pumping water into a basin.

"What in hades happened?" he asked at the same time, Reuben demanded of the reporter, "What in hell are you doing here?"

Hawk placed Sage gently in a chair pushed up against the counter.

"You forgot to mention, Baylor's daughter was staying with you," George said.

"I asked you a question, pup. What are you doing here?" Reuben all but snarled. He motioned George and Hawk out of the room.

Once they were in the hallway, George said, "Montana Brown has been hired to kill her."

"Well now, too bad you didn't get word to me yesterday." He kept his voice low, instead of yelling his lungs out like he longed too.

"I just found out today."

Through the doorway, he watched Soggy bustling around covering Sage with a large towel, so that only her shoulder was visible to prying eyes, before he started washing the wound. Reuben made sure his big body blocked the doorway so George and Hawk couldn't see her.

"Only a graze," Soggy said, relief coating his voice as he gave a sharp nod to Reuben.

"Why would the bastard send someone after Sage if Baylor had backed off?" George asked, having pieced the story together from Reuben's terse explanation, as he paced in front of the door stopping in front of Hawk as Hawk craned to see Sage.

"Either Baylor thought she'd be safe here, thinking no one knew where she was at. Or he backed off and someone is playing cat and mouse with him," Hawk said.

"Yeah, maybe." Reuben turned to watch Soggy. He yanked off his hat and ran his fingers restlessly through thinning hair then jammed it back on his head. "Gonna have to get word to him and let him know what's going on. He could be anywhere. St. Louie. Washington. Or on the B&O heading for one or the other. I hear it's a two-or three-day trip. Not bad. Not bad." He sidetracked himself.

"Is she going to be all right?" Hawk broke in.

Soggy heard.

"I'm taking care of her, ain't I?" Soggy snapped.

"That being the case, I'm heading for town." Reuben wheeled on his heel. "And you two move along. Give her some privacy."

"I know who he is. I'll take care of him." Hawk's expression grim.

"My kin." And it felt damn good to at last be able to say it. "I'll take care of him." Reuben adjusted his gun belt.

"Your kin?" George asked, whipping out his notebook.

Hawk's eyes widened.

"We had a deal. Put that damn thing away."

Ignoring the reporter, Hawk said to Reuben, looking him dead in the eye, "I know what he looks like. Besides, you're not fast enough." He brushed past Reuben.

The door banged as Hawk disappeared through it.

"You bring him back to me," Reuben hollered.

And then what?" Hawk paused on the other side.

"I'm going to string him up. Right after we find out who hired him."

Hawk signaled his approval with a jerk of his chin then was gone.

George jumped up and trotted to the door.

"Now, where are you going?" Reuben demanded.

"After him."

CHAPTER 19

Rage roiled through him, much like the black clouds blotting out the sun and dulling the horizon, as he pushed Paint from a lope into a hard gallop. It took a special kind of coward to shoot a woman. And Montana Brown fit the bill. His hands tightened on the reins, causing the pinto to shake his head and snort. Hawk forced himself to loosen his grip as he swore to himself that Montana had shot his last woman.

Sage could've been lying cold and dead on the ground right now. Montana could've killed her. Blistering heat turned to icy beads on his forehead. Thank goodness Reuben was sticking to her like a tick.

A hale from behind him broke into his churning thoughts. He glanced over his shoulder but didn't slow.

It was the reporter. What the hell had Reuben been thinking? He had fully expected Reuben to place a boot up George Story's well-pressed trousers but instead he'd acted like the newspaper man was sleuthing for him. And Hawk hadn't liked the way the cub's eyes had widened then warmed when he saw Sage. Of course, he'd shown concern for a bloodied, shot-up woman, but there'd been admiration there too. Though, why in hades he should care about other men admiring her was beyond his ken. That was Reuben's problem not his.

George hollered again.

Hawk kept going.

Twenty minutes later, he reined in the pinto, foaming and blowing, to a sedate trot as he reached the outskirts of Mobeetie.

He pulled up in front of a rundown saloon. The sign over the door was cracked and fading with the solitary word Saloon on it. Half the 'n' missing. But from the rowdy sounds coming from inside, it hadn't slowed business.

The swinging doors creaked and groaned, flapping behind him as he pushed through. He took a slow look around. A chair scraped across the floor as a short, older cowboy with skin like tanned leather threw down his cards and headed for the bar. Another picked them up along with the deck and began shuffling.

He strode to the bar, his heels clomping, causing little whisps of dust to rise from the floor.

"Beer," he said when a slovenly looking, overweight bartender raised an eyebrow in his direction. When he thumped it down, Hawk asked, "You seen Montana Brown in here?"

"Nope."

Hawk took a sip of the lukewarm, foamless draught and set it back down.

A small built man, with thin white hair asked, "You looking for Brown?"

"That's right."

"You'd have better luck at the Red Horse. Saw him in there last night, askin' for Reuben Hayes' place. Didn't seem like the type Reuben usually hires." The little man spat on the floor.

"Thanks, Mister." Hawk tossed down a double eagle. "Your next drink is on me."

"Thankee." The little man gave a big grin, showing two gold front teeth.

He swung out the doors just as George headed through them. The hinges squawking loudly.

"There you are."

Hawk didn't answer, just kept walking.

"Where we headed?"

Hawk still didn't answer.

Their heels clicked against wood as they strode down the wooden planked sidewalk. A skewbald, tied to a nearby hitching post, threw up its head and knickered before burying its nose in a nearby water trough.

Hawk cut across the street, jumping back as a cowboy raced his horse through the hard-packed earth down the middle of the street, nearly knocking George on his backside. Without a word Hawk grabbed the reporter to keep him from falling then went striding into the Red Horse.

His gaze traveled around three round tables, where men stared intently at their cards, then at the bar where half a dozen cowboys leaned on discolored wood, sipping their whiskey and beer. At the far end was a hard-featured man with a scar running down the right side of his face from eyebrow to chin. Thick red hair spilled out of a black cowboy hat.

Hawk's eyes flared and heat rose behind them. He strode toward the end of the bar never taking his gaze off the hombre. As if feeling the heat of his stare, the man looked up. His gaze sharpened in recognition.

"Montana." Hawk stopped in front of him.

"Hawk. What can I do for you?"

"Step into the street."

"What a great headline," George muttered under his breath.

"I've got no problem with that, but I'm curious as to why. You have a reputation of not looking for trouble. Nor walking away from it either."

"You here on a job?"

"Might be."

"Anything to do with Reuben Hayes?"

The talk at the table died. At the mention of Reuben, ears strained.

"Indirectly."

"You into killing women now, Montana?"

Murmurs sounded in the background.

"Scaring maybe."

"Does scaring include a bullet in the shoulder?"

"Just supposing the horse shied. What if'n the bullet should have never touched her?"

"You're not even bothering to deny it."

"I'm saying what if'n, not that I did it."

Frustration rose in Hawk's gullet. "I'll ask again. What are you doing here?"

"Like I said, maybe I gotta job."

"And what would that be?" Unconsciously, his

hand went to his gun and he tapped his fingers on the holster.

"You don't really expect me to tell you who I'm working for do you?" Muddy brown eyes arrowed to Hawk's hand and narrowed. Montana let his arms drop to his sides. He flexed his fingers.

"I'd take it as a personal favor."

"Sorry, I can't oblige."

"Then maybe you'd consider moving on."

"Now why would I do that?"

"Because I'm asking nicely and not drawing down on you. Then again, it's your choice." All thoughts of taking him to Reuben forgotten in his almighty thirst for revenge.

Chairs scraped and men edged against the wall or rushed out of the saloon. The doors swinging behind them.

"You think you can take me?" Montana sneered, pushing away from the bar and facing Hawk, his legs splayed.

Hawk's attention was momentarily diverted from Montana to George who stood several feet behind Montana shaking his head violently.

Hawk clenched and unclenched his fists, every muscle in his body tight as a coiled spring. He badly wanted to take Montana down but George was right. They needed to find out who hired the gunslinger if they wanted to end the danger to Sage.

"I know I can, but today's your lucky day. You give me the name of your employer and I'll let you walk away."

"And if I don't?"

"Then I'll beat it out of you." Hawk took a step forward.

Montana made a lightning grab for his gun.

Hawk dropped, rolled and shot in one smooth movement.

Montana's legs gave and he crumpled to the floor, a red stain spreading over his heart.

"Damn," he heard George mutter over the babble of the crowd and the thundering of his heart.

The marshal came running through the door and ground to a halt at the sight of Montana laid out on the floor.

"You," the marshal took a purposeful step towards Hawk, his eyes narrowed.

"Wasn't his fault, Marshal," the barkeep spoke up.

"What happened?"

"Lots of words floating back and forth, but in the end, Hawk stepped forward with his fists extended not his gun. Montana drew down on him. He was just defending himself."

"Anybody see any different?" The marshal looked around.

"Nope it was just like Joe said. Talk was getting pretty heated and they was about to draw down, then Hawk went in with his fists," a grizzled older gent said.

"That's so, Marshal."

"That's what happened."

"Get him to the undertaker," he told the two cowboys standing closest to him. He pointed his finger at Hawk. "I don't want to see you with a smoking gun again."

Hawk said nothing.

"You understand me?"

"I do."

The marshal gave a sharp nod, turned on his heel and slammed through the swinging doors. Hawk stepped to the bar, downed his beer then wiped the back of his hand across his mouth. He tossed down a Liberty Head gold eagle.

"For the mess."

Joe nodded and slid it in the cash register.

George sidled up to him. "Tell Reuben I'm going to stay in town and nose around."

"And then what?" Hawk asked.

"I'm going to blow this wide open and bury whoever's behind it." He swung on his heel and strode out.

CHAPTER 20

"I think it's time you told me what's going on."

Sage sat in the old rocker by the fireplace. Her face white and drawn but composed. She wore a clean blue blouse and her arm was in a sling to keep from jogging her shoulder. Soggy had dug an old brown throw out from the back of the closet and placed it on her lap.

A small table, with scarred legs—courtesy of an old hound Reuben'd had years ago—sat at her elbow. A cup of hot tea, heavily laden with whiskey and sugar, on it. Next to the tea, a chipped white plate with half a dozen cinnamon rolls. The sweet aroma swirled through the room making Reuben's stomach growl.

He'd had a stiff whiskey himself and felt marginally better. Now if he could just stop the trembles in his hands. He poured another whiskey and shoved it at Soggy. The old man couldn't be more upset if he'd been shot himself. Soggy downed it in one gulp. His hands too were shaking.

"Reuben? Why were we shot at?"

He sighed and took another gulp of whiskey wishing his dang hands would stop twitching. He straightened his shoulders and looked her in the eye. "Not we, you."

"Me? Why?" She stared at him. The cup of tea halfway to her lips.

"The senator got a note threatening you. I had supposed he'd drop the bill, but maybe he didn't." He was still chewing on that. He couldn't understand why one wouldn't protect one's loved ones above all else, no matter if the whole cursed world was threatened.

"He knew you'd keep me safe," she said simply before sipping her tea. As it slid down her throat, her eyes widened then teared. She rasped out, "It certainly warms the belly." She nodded at Soggy.

"Supposed to," he said grumpily.

"But I didn't." The words ripped out of his throat and he'd swear he felt the tear all the way from his heart.

"You have, you know," she said calmly before taking another cautious sip of tea then settling back in the rocker. "If you hadn't knocked me off the horse, there's no telling what would have happened. Life isn't without risks."

"The senator needs to backoff on this." He clenched his fists then forced himself to relax them.

"Let Daddy do his job. You'll keep me safe."

"How can you say that when a bullet bit into your shoulder?"

"Grazed my shoulder."

Before he could say more the main door slammed and Hawk came stomping in, his features grim. As if drawn, his gaze arrowed to Sage. What he saw must have reassured him because he relaxed marginally.

Reuben looked over his shoulder. "Where is he?"

"Getting measured for a pine box."

"I told you—"

Hawk cut in. "He didn't give me a choice."

"What did you find out?"

"He was only supposed to scare her."

"Who sent him?"

"Don't know. He didn't talk." Red rode up his collar and frustration flashed across his face.

It also showed on Reuben's. "Then why did you shoot him?"

"'Cause he was going to shoot me," Hawk shouted, losing his composure completely.

"Sometimes you have to make sacrifices," Soggy said, though his eyes twinkled.

"You're saying I should have let him shoot me?"

Soggy shrugged, his eyes still glinting, shrugged again and repeated, "Sometimes you got to make sacrifices."

Seeing the ridiculous in the situation, Reuben calmed. Though it took an effort. "Where's George?"

"He's nosing around town. Seeing if he can find out anything." Hawk too calmed, realizing Soggy was funning him.

"I think I'll just mosey in town myself." Reuben downed the rest of his whiskey and thumped it on the table at Sage's elbow. He pointed a finger at Sage.

"Give me an hour or so to get guards set up around the perimeter of the house. After that you don't leave the house, even to go to the privy, without two of us with you."

"You rigged up a water closet in the house, remember? Probably the only one in Texas."

His stubble rasped as he rubbed his chin. He was right proud of his water closet. And Sage was right it was probably the only one in Texas, unless Brandon Wade had one.

Reuben and Soggy had rigged up a gravity fed system, with basic clay piping and dug a cesspit. It had taken them the better part of a year to get the kinks worked out, but by goldurn they'd done it.

"It was just a figure of speech. But if you go out for any reason, Hawk and Soggy go with you.

"Got that?" He looked at each person in the room. When each had nodded, he turned on his heel and headed for the door, calling over his shoulder, "Remember to wait an hour before you head outside or to the barn. Give me time to get men in place. And wear a hat to cover that shiny chestnut mane. No point in giving anyone something to aim at."

The door banged behind him as he strode through it, his heels clopping on wooden planks as he trotted off the porch and down the steps. Frustration sat like a hard rock in his craw. He'd taken the situation serious alright, but not seriously enough. Hadn't realized someone would ferret out her location or have the temerity to take a potshot at her while she was with him. Well, that was about to change.

His jaw tightened. He was going to have to hire more men. A small army if need be. And she wouldn't be leaving the property unless several men were riding with her and the area scoped out in advance.

He untied the reins that were wrapped around the hitching post and jumped into the saddle then trotted to the barn and called out, "Billy."

"Yeah, boss," the young man dropped the bale he was carrying and came hurrying out.

"Go to the bunkhouse and get a rifle. From now on, I want either you or Levi up at the house, on the porch, at all times, except when you're relieved."

Billy gave a nod his expression serious.

"How's Miss Sage?"

Word had got round pretty quick that his boss's guest had been attacked.

"She's going to be fine and we're going to keep her that way. Right?"

"Right."

Reuben wheeled his horse and headed to the range, the Appaloosa's hooves crushing new grass, causing the scent of fresh to rise up and settle in the thick broody air that hung over the ranch.

Twenty minutes later, he reached the herd.

Reining in his horse, he stood in the stirrup, cupped his hand around his mouth and called, "Levi."

On the other side of the herd, Levi came galloping toward him accompanied by the sounds of lowing and mooing. He reined in next to Reuben.

"Boss."

"Levi, I need you back at the house."

"You know that'll just leave Henry and Slim with the herd."

"I'm going in town to hire more help. I want you to ride herd on the perimeter of the ranch."

"What's going on?"

"Sage is in danger."

"What?" His black sidled as Levi jerked on the reins.

Reuben didn't repeat himself. Figured he didn't need to.

"You can count on me."

"I do," Reuben turned his horse.

"How many you hiring?"

"At least three. More'n if I can get 'em."

"The barkeep's got a nephew, youngish, barely fifteen, but he could herd the cattle."

"Thanks. I'll check on him." Reuben touched heels to flanks and headed for town. Levi took off in the opposite direction.

He pushed his horse hard. The animal's big body bunching and uncoiling beneath him. By the time he reached Mobeetie, the Appaloosa was foam-flecked and blowing. Reuben tied him to the hitching post in front of the Red Horse and strode in, the doors swinging behind him.

"Beer," he told Joe, leaning on the bar, the scents of yeasty alcohol, sawdust and plain ole sweat wafting over him.

Joe slapped a foaming mug in front of him.

"I hear you have a nephew that might be looking for work." Reuben took a long pull, thumped the glass down and wiped his mouth.

"Mayhap. What ya got in mind?"

"Cattle work. Rucking out stalls. The usual around a ranch."

"Any gun work?" Joe narrowed his eyes.

"I can't guarantee there won't be, but I'll keep him in the background. I'm hiring to free up my own men in case there is any gunfire exchanged."

"This got anything to do with Hawk killin' Montana Brown?"

"Yeah, it does."

"Is it true Montana tried to kill that young woman staying with you?"

"Well, I can't say if he was trying to kill her or not, but he shot her sure enough." He ground his teeth. Just thinking about it made him mad all over again.

Joe who'd been drying a glass scrubbed harder, his lips a thin straight line. "It takes a special kind of lowdown sidewinder to shoot a woman."

"That it does." Reuben rocked back on his heels.

"Well, the boy could use the work, and my sister the money. I'll send him out."

"I'd appreciate it."

"When do you want him?"

"Yesterday."

Reuben took a long look around. His gaze came to rest on a table of poker players. Most of them he knew. He straightened and strode toward them.

"Lo, boys."

"Reuben."

"Mr. Hayes."

Eyes lifted briefly then went back to their cards.

"Anybody looking for work?"

"Let you know after this hand," a man, with a red bandana wrapped around his neck said. Jose did odd jobs around town and occasionally filled in on the ranches when someone needed an extra hand.

"I'll be at the bar." Reuben moseyed back to the bar. His steps and posture not revealing the tension and rage that roiled through him. The only giveaway, the heat snapping behind his eyes.

He leaned an elbow on the bar, his faded blue, woven wool vest sliding against the high gloss of the long wood counter. Then glanced at the wide mirror behind it that reflected the image of anyone that came through the door. He crossed his boots and sipped his beer. With one last look at the reflection of the swinging doors, he turned his attention to the card game just in time to see Jose throw down his cards and come stomping toward him, his expression resigned.

"What's your nephew's name, Joe?" he asked the barkeep that was rubbing the counter down, buffing it till Reuben could see his reflection. Something he'd rather not do. With the broken nose and various scars, it was a face only a mother could love.

"Abe. Abe Ellis. A tall gawky kid."

"Send him to Levi. He'll put him to work."

"Will do. I'll send someone over to tell him right away. He could have had a job here sweeping floors and emptying chew pots, but his mother thinks he's too good for that." He snorted.

"How's she going to feel about her boy working odd jobs on a ranch." Reuben's eyebrows rose.

"For Reuben Hayes? She'll be dining out on that for weeks." He shook his head and rubbed harder at the counter.

Reuben snorted.

"Mr. Hayes." Jose stood beside him. He took off his hat but looked him in the eye.

"Lost did ya?"

"I did."

Reuben chewed on a grin, briefly reminded of Hawk. Cards were sure sending ranch hands his way.

"When can you start?"

"Now soon enough?"

"Now works. Head on out and report to Levi. Tell him I sent you."

"Will do." He nodded, pushed thick black hair off his forehead that flopped back down, and shoved his hat on.

As he turned, a cowboy dressed in black, pushed up and started toward them.

"I wouldn't trust him," Jose said in a low tone before stomping to the door.

Even from the distance between them, Reuben could see the thin line of the mouth and the shift in brown eyes and figured Jose was right.

"So you hirin'?" The cowboy came to a stop in front of him, his expression insolent, his lip curled and his hand resting on his gun.

"I was looking for a cowpuncher. You don't look like no cowpuncher." Reuben's gaze slid to the hombre's hand resting on his gun then back up to his face.

"You saying I can't punch a dumb cow?"

"I'm wonderin' why you want to."

"Maybe I'm broadening my horizons."

"Don't matter. I just filled the position."

"Maybe you don't like the way I look." He took a step closer. Close enough Reuben smelled sour and booze on his breath and saw the hot, eager gleam in his eyes.

"Mayhap I don't." Reuben straightened, putting him over six-one, with twice the bulk of the stranger in front of him.

"Mister, if you've got a lick of sense, which I'm not sure in your case you do, I wouldn't go out of my way to rile Reuben Hayes," the bartender said.

The cowboy sneered, spit at the copper spittoon on the floor and missed.

Reuben eyed the spittle on the floor then said to Joe in conversational tones, "Mayhap your sister has a point."

"Mayhap she does."

The hombre, tired of being ignored, drilled a finger into his Reuben's chest. "You don't scare me, ole man."

"Now ya done it," Joe muttered and stepped back as far as the space behind the bar would allow.

For a bulky man, Reuben was lightning. He grabbed the man's arm and with the other thumped him face down on the gleaming counter.

"I've had a really bad day." Hot blood coursed through his system, like a caged wolf waiting to be released.

The man's hat fell off and Reuben yanked him up by his hair and planted his fist between the hombre's eyes. The hombre went down like he'd been pole-axed.

"Get up."

If the hombre heard him, he kept his eyes tightly shut.

"Get up," Reuben growled again and toed him none too gently with a pointed cowboy boot.

The man groaned but made no move to comply. Reuben hauled him to his feet and half-carried, half-dragged him to the door, finishing the journey with a boot to the man's backside.

The hombre fell through the swinging doors, his body blocking the sidewalk, his head hanging over it into the street.

Reuben felt marginally better. A good dustup had that effect.

"I'll be on the lookout for your nephew, Joe, and try to keep him out of harm's way."

"Good luck with that. Trouble follows you like an old hound dog, Reuben." Joe shook his head.

Reuben gave Joe an abbreviated wave, pushed through the door and mounted his Appaloosa. As he started to ride out a scuffle behind him had him reaching for his gun as he whirled in the saddle.

The marshal was wrestling a gun out of the man's hand Reuben had just bested and had his boot squarely on the man's back. He tossed the gun into the street and slapped on cuffs.

"This one's on me," the marshal called.

"Thankee, John."

John gave a jerk of his chin in acknowledgement.

His horse kicking up dirt, Reuben trotted down the street heading out of town. He'd gotten as far as the boardinghouse when he realized he hadn't spoken to George. With a sigh, he reined his horse in. Might as well start here.

He tied the Appaloosa to a hitching post and went striding in, a bell over the door jingling merrily.

Agatha looked up from the ledger she was studying. Her hair pulled back in a tight gray bun, wearing a serviceable beige dress, she stood behind a counter that would put Joe's gleaming bar to shame. No self-respecting dust mote would dare dance through her spotless window. The walls were covered in yellow-flowered silk wallpaper that he found a bit fussy, though he liked it better than the pink she used to have up. But all in all, Agatha ran a bang-up boardinghouse.

"Reuben." Her stern features relaxed in a smile that lifted her lips and put a twinkle in her brown eyes.

"Agatha." He doffed his hat.

"What can I do for you?"

"Have you seen that young reporter feller?"

"He's staying here."

"Can I have his room number?"

"You may, but it won't do you any good. He just stepped out."

Of course. He fought off a sigh. Finding him here on his first try would have been too easy and if there was one thing Reuben knew to be as true as the sun rising in the east, life wasn't easy.

"I don't suppose you know where he's going?" he asked without much hope.

She gave him what in a younger woman would

have been a flirtatious smile, leaned across the counter and lowered her voice as if to impart a secret. The wafting scent of rose water had his nose twitching.

"That young man is on the trail of a story."

"Oh yeah? What makes you say that?" He just managed not to give a start, though his belly had sure jumped. Instead, he leaned in.

Nothing could have pleased her more than his reaction. She now had his full attention.

She looked right then left and whispered loudly, "He's asking questions."

Reuben managed not to roll his eyes, just. "He's a reporter. That's what they do."

She gave him an irritated look. "Yes, but it's the questions he's asking."

"And what might they be?"

"He's still asking about Senator Baylor. Now why would he do that, if there's not something brewing? And he's asking about new people that have come to town.

"Mr. Dekker says he's over there everyday nattering at him on who's had or sent a telegram. Well now, Mr. Dekker told him in no uncertain terms he couldn't give him that information. So he's taken to sitting in the office, seeing who comes in or goes out. He's a cagey one." She shook her head, an admiring expression on her face.

"In fact, that's where he's gone." She looked at the watch pinned to her scrawny bosom. "Near six o'clock. I'd think Mr. Dekker would be closing up."

"I better hurry then. I thankee."

"Anytime, Reuben. Anytime."

He shoved his hat down on his head, tipped it in her direction then stomped through the door, the bell once again jangling.

He strode down the walk, his heels clicking. Then took a smart step to his right as a ball—once bright red and now dulled with dust—two boys were hitting back and forth with a stick, came rolling toward him. As it headed for the street, he spun it back with a tap of his boot.

"Thanks, Mr. Hayes," the tallest of the two, with tufts of blond hair sticking out all over his head, called as he caught it and bounced it along.

Five minutes later, Reuben reached the telegraph office. He looked at the "Closed" sign and swore. Hand above eyes, he peered in the window in the hopes Mr. Dekker was still inside. Everything was closed up tight. The only movement, a mouse scurrying across the floor.

"Dang." He took off his hat, slapped it against his leg, shoved it back on and headed for the closest saloon.

By the time he trudged back to the boarding house, the sun had set. He'd been in all eight saloons and in most of them the message was the same. "Just missed him."

"Hell with it." He reached for his horse's reins, wrapped around the rail, then paused. He needed to get home and check on his daughter. He also needed to track down who was behind this heinous attack on her. Soggy, Hawk and Levi would keep her safe.

Rubbing his chin, he stared at the boardinghouse. He'd just poke his head in. If George wasn't there he'd hie on home and wait to hear from him.

The bell tinkled as he stepped inside.

Agatha looked up from the customer she was checking in and pointed upstairs.

"What room?" Reuben asked.

"Two-fourteen."

"My room number is two-fourteen?" the little man standing in front of her asked.

"No, sir, you are in two-ten."

Reuben gave her a nod and a half-salute and went trotting up the stairs, turned to the right and pounded his big fist against the door of 214.

Shuffling sounded on the other side of the door before George threw it open.

A bright blue carpetbag sat on the rose-colored duvet on the high poster bed.

"Going somewhere?" Reuben asked in a dry voice.

"Washington, DC. Taking the stage first thing tomorrow," George responded and stepped away from the door.

Reuben's jaw went slack. When he recovered, he asked, "And when were you going to let me know about this?"

George pointed at an envelope, propped up against the plain white pitcher on his dresser with Reuben's name on it.

"I'm not getting anywhere here, but I think I can blast this thing wide open in Washington. It's where it started and where it's going to end." Fire lit his eyes, his face flushed, fervor in his voice.

"You got enough money to get you there?"

"I planned on charging my expenses to you." George gave him an impudent grin.

"I guess that's fair." Reuben thrust his hands in his back pockets and rocked on his heels.

"While you're here, I've got a few questions."

"And what questions would you have for me?"

"Why is Sage Baylor visiting you?"

"Don't see as how that's any of your business." Then relented. "I'm an old friend of her mother."

"How good a friend? When I was at the ranch, you said Sage Baylor was kin." George watched him closely, his eyes alert. But not closely enough.

Reuben grabbed him by his shirt collar, lifted him, till they were nose to nose.

"Again, I don't see's how that's any of your business."

George pointed with a finger to his throat and wheezed, "Can't breathe."

Reuben gave him a last shake then set him on his feet, glaring at him.

George gasped, trying to get his breathing regulated.

"Do you have any leads?"

"Maybe," George managed to get out.

"What?"

"I'd rather not say until I have more facts to back it up." He took a cautious step back.

"Fair enough. Have you heard about anyone else in

town or coming to town that would harm Sage?"

"I haven't. But if I do, I promise you. I promise you," he repeated. "I will send you a telegram letting you know."

"You see Baylor, you tell him to back off that bill for a while."

"I don't think he'll do that, sir." He rubbed his throat and watched Reuben cautiously.

"I don't understand. You take care of your own before anyone else." Reuben walked to the window and looked into the gathering gloom, his hands in his back pockets.

"Sir, if she was with anyone else, he might, and I emphasize might, back off of this, but the way he'll see it is many lives are at stake, innocent lives, and if she's not safe with you, she's not safe anywhere."

"I can't agree with him on this." Reuben watched a scrawny cat skulk along the sidewalk then disappear into an alley.

"I can't say as I agree or disagree, but I understand, and thank goodness my job is to remain objective and not color the story."

"It's more than a story to some, young man. It's more than a story to me."

"And that's what makes you a legend."

"I'm no legend." Reuben gave a derisive snort.

"Even in St. Louis, I'd heard of Reuben Hayes. Killed more men, fought more Indians, and hung more rustlers than anyone in the West. Larger than life stuff. In fact, after this is said and done, I'd love to have an interview and write your story."

Reuben shook his head and swung around. "I can double damn guarantee it's a lot less colorful than what you've heard."

"Then maybe it's a story that needs to be told."

"You help save my—" He paused and cleared his throat. "You find out who's behind these attempts on Sage's life, we'll discuss it."

George stepped up and held out his hand.

"You got a deal."

CHAPTER 21

Three weeks to the day since Reuben had shaken hands on a deal with George, young Jinks again came riding hell for leather onto the ranch with another telegram.

"Go grab a cup of coffee," Reuben told Levi who was on porch duty, while Billy rode the ranch's parameters.

"You sure?"

"I think I can handle young Jinks," he said dryly. Stepping off the porch to meet him, Reuben held out his hand as Levi disappeared into the house.

Jinks handed him the telegram.

Paper crinkled as the words leaped off the paper.

She's still in danger and so is the senator. It's bigger than I thought. Ever heard of the KKK?

It wasn't signed. It didn't need to be.

The sun sank, haloing horse and rider, turning the telegram a deep bloody red, before it wavered then dropped in a graceful arc on the horizon.

"Thanks, Jinks," Reuben said, his mind on the words jumping off the paper and straight into his gullet. He tossed the young man a coin.

Jinks nodded, reined his horse in a circle and

galloped off into the gathering gloom. The sound of hooves thudded against hard-packed earth, strong then growing fainter before disappearing altogether, leaving only the snap of wind through a nearby oak's branches.

Fury, fierce and blistering, surged through him, burning down to his toes. The telegram crackled as his big paw crunched it into a ball.

The door banged as Soggy came out, wiping his hands on the flour-spattered towel wrapped around his waist, his small pooch hanging over it.

"Who was that?"

"Young Jinks."

Soggy held out his hand.

"It may be something that's none of your business," Reuben said, more out of habit than anything else. The two men had known each other too long for there to be any secrets between them.

Soggy said nothing, just waited.

With a sigh, Reuben dropped the wadded-up telegram into it.

Soggy straightened out the paper and squinted. Reuben pulled his spectacles out of one of his vest pockets and handed them to his cook.

Soggy pushed them on his nose and scanned the missive. "Is that the group that don't like ole Moses' kind and runs around in sheets?"

Moses had been considerably older than Soggy and shown up one morning after the war. He'd been competent and loyal, and played a mean harmonica. He'd up and died a year ago and both men felt the loss.

"Yeah."

"And tell me again what that has to do with our Sage and the senator?"

The 'our' notched down the rage. Like himself, Soggy would keep her safe or die trying. "The senator is trying to pass an anti-lynching bill."

"I've never understood that level of hate."

"Some people have to push others down to pull themselves up." He shrugged. Color didn't matter much to him. Over the years he'd hired white, black, red, yellow and shades of brown. It was what the man was made of that mattered. As long as they pulled their weight and minded their own business that was good enough for him.

"Sure wish the senator would back off. I'd rest easier," Reuben said.

"Mayhap he knows it wouldn't make no difference now. That whoever is behind this is determined to punish him for going against 'em. And what better punishment than killing his kin."

Reuben pulled air in through his nose then blew it out as the fury in him turned hot as red coals again, burning him from the inside out.

"Now who in tarnation is that?"

The question had Reuben wheeling and looking toward the dirt trail as a stranger rode under the HAYES RANCH sign.

The door banged and Levi came meandering out, his gait easy, his gaze alert.

"Don't recognize the horse," Reuben said, as he studied the distinctive piebald with a solid black head.

"You, Levi?"

"Nope."

The three men had shifted till they stood shoulder to shoulder.

"Hawk," Reuben called over his shoulder.

The door swung open and Hawk stepped out.

Reuben heard the lighter steps clicking behind Hawk's brisker ones.

"Stay inside, missy."

For a wonder she obeyed.

"Recognize that horse or the man on its back?"

Hawk's gaze arrowed on the rider.

"Nope."

A board creaked as Hawk moved in front of the door, his body blocking Sage. Reuben gave a sharp nod of approval.

The horse snorted and tossed his head as the rider hauled on the reins, halting his mount in front of the porch, shadowed in the twilight.

"What can I do for you, stranger?" Reuben asked, his hand casually on his gun. The man started to dismount.

"That's far enough."

The man straightened and settled back into the saddle. He lifted his arms to show he wasn't packing.

"I heard in town you were hiring."

"What town would that be?"

"Mobeetie."

"Don't recall seeing you in town."

"Just got in."

"You must be in an almighty hurry for a job."

"Can't afford a hotel. Or a meal for that matter." He gave a rueful laugh.

"Get down and let me have a look at you."

The stranger swung his leg over his saddle and tied the piebald to the hitching post then stepped onto the porch. He stopped in the muted light from the doorway that outlined Hawk and shimmered around him.

The stranger wore blue canvas pants and a faded blue plaid shirt. Medium height and about Hawk's age, Reuben guessed. His expression was congenial enough, but behind light brown eyes lurked something sharp, reminiscent of a bird of prey, perfectly motionless as it waited for its unsuspecting quarry.

Reuben reached out and grabbed his hands.

"Hey." The man gave him a startled look.

Reuben ran his rough thumb over the man's fingertips.

"Unless you want to dance, I suggest you drop my hands." The words were said lightly but there was a world of warning behind them.

Hawk stiffened.

Reuben dropped them and hitched up his pants.

"Well now, I don't suppose you're talking about do-si-doing and you don't use a gun, so I'm not sure what kind of dancing you got in mind."

"You're a smart one. Figured out I didn't have a gun from the feel of my hands?"

"No calluses on your trigger finger or your middle finger near the pad where a gun would fit. Knife man maybe."

"Maybe. Man has to be able to protect himself somehow."

Something didn't set right. The hombre was hiding something. And there was a slickness about him Reuben didn't like. And what self-respecting cowboy didn't carry a gun?

Still, they needed help.

Minutes passed. The silence unbroken as he mulled it over.

If he kept the hombre out on the range and away from the house, it should be all right. Plus, he could keep an eye on him.

"Your call, Levi."

Levi gave the stranger a long once over. Finally, he said, "We could use a man on the range. Free up Jose to keep the stables rucked and the horses fed.

"Maybe have young Abe do the rucking and leave Jose on the range." Abe would be safe enough in the stables.

"Young Abe it is then."

"Well, stranger. Looks like you've got yourself a job."

"Thankee."

"Levi will show you where to bunk down at and Soggy'll bring you something to eat. Tomorrow morning you can ride out to the range with Jose."

"All right."

"You got a name?"

"Smith. John Smith."

CHAPTER 22

"John Smith, my—" Hawk looked at Sage and his voice trailed off.

"Yeah," Reuben said. He came inside, the door slamming behind him as Levi took the new hire to the bunkhouse. The smell of the roast and potatoes they'd had for dinner still lingering in the air as he strode through the hall into the living area.

"What did the telegram say?" Sage lit the kerosene lamp and looked in its light—to Reuben's way of thinking—bright as a new minted penny. She wore a turquoise and white plaid shirt, a black divided skirt and Western boots, with swirls of turquoise along the shaft, that he had harangued the bootmaker into making in a short amount of time. Course, a couple of double eagles over and above the asking price hadn't hurt any.

"Is Dad okay?"

"Yes, but you are both still in danger." He clenched his fists and shoved them in his pockets, still fighting the fury.

"Do you know who from?" Her expression calm, only the rapid pulse in her throat and the color riding high in her cheeks gave her away. He knew the anxiety was not for herself.

"He's going to be okay."

"You can't guarantee that."

"No. I can't. But he strikes me as a man too determined to die."

"Thank you." She gave a little laugh, reached up and kissed him on the cheek.

It rocked him down to his boots and it was all he could do not to grab her to him and hold tight. He'd missed so much. Her birth. Her first steps. Her formative years. But she was here now, he reminded himself. Take the present and don't worry about the past or future. When she would leave him like her momma had. He shook it off.

She stepped back.

"What was that for?"

She shook her head and smiled.

"Well, whatever the reason, I'll take it." He gave her a crooked grin, glanced over and saw Soggy scrubbing vigorously at his eyes. He hitched an eyebrow. Soggy shot up his chin and gave him a pugnacious look as if daring him to say something. And looked like nothing so much as an aging bantam rooster.

He turned his attention back to his daughter.

"Stay away from John Smith."

"You don't trust him."

"Not a bit."

"Then why'd you hire him?"

Chestnut curls fell to the side of her shoulder as she tipped her head to study him. Her expression inquiring.

"Keep your friends close. Keep your enemies closer."

"This way you can keep an eye on him."

He nodded.

"Do you know who my dad's in danger from?" she repeated.

"Only that it's someone linked to the Ku Klux Klan."

She wandered over and sank down on the arm of the worn leather sofa filled with horsehair and wool padding.

"That makes things a bit challenging, doesn't it?"

"Yeah, it does. The clan is built on secrecy. Anybody could hide behind it." He glanced at Hawk who prowled the room as restless as a young cougar that couldn't settle.

"Got something on your mind, Hawk?"

"Ever heard of Jack Santos?"

CHAPTER 23

Tension built.

Silence stretched.

Finally, Reuben said in his gravelly voice, "I've heard of him."

"He the knife thrower?" Soggy asked.

"Yeah," Both Reuben and Hawk responded.

"And you think that boyo who looks more like a farmer than a rancher is him?" Soggy started to spit on the floor, remembered where he was and swallowed.

Reuben eyed Hawk, "Do you?"

"I've never seen him. He keeps a low profile. Except for his reputation. He can't stop that from growing. And there's something off about John Smith."

"I haven't heard of him." The sofa arm sighed as Sage stood.

"He's a hired gun," Hawk replied.

"But he doesn't carry a gun."

"I misspoke. He's a hired killer."

"Without a gun?"

"He's a knife man. They say his knife can whizz past a speeding bullet."

"They," she emphasized, "say a lot of things."

"Reuben?" she asked, when he didn't respond.

"He's dangerous. I'd rather face a hired gun." Hands in pockets he looked out the window into the darkening night then turned to Hawk. "And you think John Smith is Jack Santos?"

"It would make sense, wouldn't it? No one knows what he looks like. He's a chameleon. He assumes a different identity with each job." Hawk stopped his pacing and asked, "Do you want me to move him along?"

There was a wealth of meaning behind his words.

Reuben once again turned back to the window and the dark beyond it, his hands still resting in his back pockets. Finally, he swung around. "Yes."

"You sure about this?"

"I'm sure." His muscles taut. His skin tight. His lips thinned.

With an abrupt nod, Hawk headed for the door.

"What are you two talking about?" Sage asked.

Neither man answered.

She leaped forward and planted herself in front of the door before Hawk could reach it.

"You're going to kill him?" Tinged with disbelief, her voice rose along with her eyebrows.

"Step aside, Sage." Hawk stopped in front of her.

In answer, she threw her hands out and grasped the doorframe.

"I'm not going to let you do this. You don't even know if it's the same man. You could be killing an innocent."

"I'm willing to risk it," Reuben said.

"And you?" She looked at Hawk.

His silence was answer enough.

"Soggy?" She turned to the cook, her expression imploring.

He looked uncomfortable but lifted his chin and said calmly, "I stand with Reuben."

"Against me."

"For you."

She shook her head and notched her chin. "My daddy would never do this."

"No, he wouldn't. But your father would and will."

Hawk blinked and his jaw dropped before he got his expression back under control.

"I won't forgive you, if you do this." Her gaze went unerringly to Reuben's.

Regret shot through him. Acid spurted in his belly, but all he said was, "I'll live with that."

She changed her tack.

"Please."

He opened his mouth to say no. Nothing came out.

He tried to shake his head. That didn't work either.

Finally, he managed to get words past his dry throat. "You do realize John Smith could be here to kill you."

"Surely, no mousy-looking little man is going to get past the three of you?"

"Mousy can be a pretty damn good disguise for a killer."

"But whoever is behind this is trying to scare me not kill me."

"The stakes could go up anytime. What we're

dealing with are fanatics."

"I'll be careful. I won't go anywhere without one of you with me. Please," she repeated.

There were no female histrionics. No begging or pleading, just looking him in the eye and uttering that one word. And that was his undoing.

"No more riding out. You'll have to limit yourself to the house."

"And the barn. I'll need to check on Thunder and Darling."

"Two of us will have to go with you when you do."

Her eyes twitched but she didn't roll them.

"All right."

He glanced at Hawk, whose face was carefully blank. Whatever he was thinking, he was keeping it to himself.

"How about now?" she asked.

"Now, what?"

"I'd like to go to the barn to see my horses."

He bit back a grin at her possessive tone.

"Can't it wait till morning?"

"It could. But I haven't seen them today and they'll be wondering where I'm at."

"Let's go. Hawk." Out of the corner of his eye he caught Soggy shaking his head. Ignoring it, he grabbed a lantern, lit it and they headed to the stable.

Billy was carrying a bale of hay to the far end of the building where Thunder and Darling were stalled.

"You and Hawk keep an eye on Miss Sage will you, Billy. You guard her with your life and do exactly what Hawk tells you." Billy didn't have Hawk's particular set of skills, but he was loyal. Loyal enough to throw himself in front of a knife if need be.

"Yes, sir." His chest swelled as he dropped the bale of hay he was hauling and hurried toward them. The earthy scent of dried grass, rising along with dust and bits of pulverized weeds floating in the air, accompanied the thump.

"Thank you," Sage said.

Reuben nodded and strode back toward the house, his heels digging in the dirt.

The door slammed as he entered the house, grabbed a cup of coffee and downed it, thinking he needed something stronger. "I'll be on the porch till Levi gets John Smith settled in.

"What?" he demanded at Soggy's knowing look.

"I didn't say a word. Not one word." Soggy threw up his hands and went back to his dishes.

CHAPTER 24

Days passed.

John Smith slipped into the ranch's rhythms without a ripple. The hands had relaxed around him. But Hawk kept his guard up. And Soggy and Reuben didn't relax around anyone.

Reuben had spread the word that he, Hawk, had come down with a mysterious malady and was bunking in Soggy's room behind the kitchen where a spare bed was kept for anyone sick and in need of Soggy's services. Reuben and Levi guarded Sage during the day and Hawk at night. He kept watch from a hard-backed chair placed in the shadows where he could see anyone come through the door.

Fighting sleep, he trudged into the kitchen and put his head under the pump. A sharp breeze blowing through the open window hit the wet of his face and revived him.

The cool night wind carried the hoot of an owl from a nearby tree followed by a flap of wings. Seconds later, a small creature squealed.

A rodent in his mouth, the owl flew away, outlined by a moon that traveled in and out of dark clouds. By its location in the sky, Hawk guessed it must be nearing midnight. He pulled out his watch for confirmation. Ten minutes till. Another five hours before anyone would be awake and stirring.

He reached for a mug in the pantry to pour himself a cold, stout cup of coffee. Then froze as the door creaked. Loud in the quiet.

The hairs on the back of his neck lifted. A chill spread through his bones.

Silently, he reached for his gun. It wasn't impossible that it was Billy, keeping watch on the porch, but it was unlikely. Last man up, in the bunkhouse, always brought Billy, or whoever was on watch, a cup of coffee.

Quiet as a cat, he put his heels down then rolled his feet forward till his toes were on the ground.

No one was in the entryway or living room. Whoever was in the house moved with the stealth of a fox.

A dark shape shifted in the hallway. The bastard might be as quiet as ghost but he couldn't control his shadow crawling up the wall, Hawk thought with savage satisfaction.

Heels thumped against the wood floor, along with the snick of his gun hammer, as Hawk leaped forward.

At the sound, silver flashed. The knife whistled in the dark.

He jerked to the side, slamming against the wall.

The knife whizzed by him, slicing his arm before it clattered to the floor, along with his gun.

Warm, sticky liquid spurted. His heart galloped and his blood rushed through his system. For a moment, he felt a sharp burn, then raw power kicked in and he felt nothing but the savage pleasure of plunging his fist in Jack Santos' face as he collided with the shadowy figure in front of him, taking him to the ground.

That it was Santos, going by the name Smith, he had no doubt. The sleek body, the lack of gun calluses on his hands as they struggled gave him away. The hall too dark to make out features other than outlines and whites of eyes.

Doors banged against walls as they were thrown open. He tuned out the distraction, all his attention focused on his opponent. The man beneath him slippery as an eel.

He managed to plant his fist between Santos' eyes. His assailant took the blow, grunting. They grappled. It was all he could do to keep his hold on the would-be killer as they rolled back and forth. One minute him on top. One minute Santos. Again, his body clonked against the wall. He rolled. Got Santos by the hair and thumped his head on the floor.

Santos lifted him with his feet and flipped him. Hawk's back thudded against the floor.

"Hawk, watch out." He dimly heard Sage's shriek as she jumped on Santos' back trying to pull him off. Santos back-handed her, knocking her off and pulled out another knife from his belt.

Reuben reached for Santos just as Sage flew backwards taking them both to the floor. Boards shook as Reuben landed with a thud, Sage on top of him.

Anger fueled Hawk. Ignoring the arm across his throat cutting off his air, he grasped Santos' wrist and squeezed. Santos held on, breathing hard. His eyes bright and hungry.

Fury roiled through Hawk's system and biting his teeth together, he increased the pressure. Harder. Harder. Until the knife clattered from Santos' fingers.

Quick as a striking snake, Hawk grabbed the knife and plunged it into Santos' heart. The man's eyes widened in surprise before he slumped on top of Hawk.

Hawk scrambled out from under him.

Light from a kerosene lamp bobbed as Soggy shoved aside Reuben and Sage who were now on their feet.

"What the hell is going on?" he demanded.

CHAPTER 25

Breathing heavily, blood covering him, Hawk pushed to his feet.

Everyone converged around him. His gaze arrowed straight to Sage as she ran her hands up and down his arms. "Are you alright?" she asked.

His ears rang from the head thumping. The sharp stinging pain in his arm now throbbed like a kettle drum and aches that he hadn't noticed during the fight were cropping up all over his body. Even his hair hurt. "I'm fine. Are you alright?"

"Thanks to you."

"It seems I'm in your debt again." Reuben grabbed the hand of Hawk's bad arm and pumped.

Hawk winced. Reuben noticed and dropped his hand.

"Move now. Let me see the boy." The lantern in Soggy's hand threw shadows that flickered and danced on the white-washed wall as he pushed the other two aside and kicked the lifeless body out of his way.

"I go to the privy in the middle of the night and all hell breaks loose. You hurt anywhere else?" Soggy lifted the lantern and peered at Hawk's arm.

Hawk's blood slogged through his system, except what was steadily dripping down his arm. Tiredness hit him like a sledgehammer.

"You hurt anywhere else?" Soggy repeated, his gaze still on Hawk's arm as he poked around the edges of the slash.

"Mmph." Hawk grunted as Soggy's poking fingers shot another round of pain through his system. "No."

"How did he get past Billy?" Reuben demanded as they shuffled out of the hallway. "I better check on him."

The door slammed and they heard him bellow, "Billy."

"Get yourself to the kitchen," Soggy commanded Hawk before he trotted after Reuben, the light from the lantern doing a crazy dance in the dark. Hawk motioned Sage forward as she hesitated, reaching a hand out toward him. "I'm fine. See about Billy." She hesitated. He gave her a reassuring smile, straightened and forced himself to put one foot in front of the other as he ignored Soggy's instructions and stumbled after them.

"Billy, wake up." Reuben grabbed him by his vest and shook him.

Billy gave a snort in response, a puddle of drool forming at the side of his mouth. A cup lay on its side, spilled coffee staining the porch in a splotchy pool.

"He's been drugged." Reuben's eyebrows shot up along with his voice. He let go off Billy and whipped around. "I'll get that worthless polecat out of the house. Soggy see to Hawk."

"Could have sworn that's what I was about to do," Soggy grumbled. "Come on."

Hawk trailed behind the cook as Sage trotted about lighting the lamps. The one in the kitchen outlined her lithe form shining through a pristine white nightgown that covered her from neck to ankles. Hawk cleared his throat. Soggy followed his gaze.

"Girl, better get dressed or at least throw on a robe."

Catching Hawk's gaze, red crept up her collar and landed in her cheeks. She nodded and disappeared, as a sliding sound followed by a thump, came from the living area. A door slammed. A dark-red, smeared trail left behind.

Hawk watched Soggy pump water into a granite basin, liquid splashing into the sink and onto the sideboard. Finally, he said with a tinge of laughter in his voice, "Uh, maybe you should throw on some pants before you start working on me, with Sage in the house and all."

Soggy glanced down at the red long johns covering his scrawny legs.

"Humph. I suppose you're right. Sit." He pointed a bony finger at the already sitting Hawk. In response, Hawk just laid his head on the table and closed his eyes. He heard the door slam and Soggy say, "Appears we both need to throw on some clothes."

"Yeah," Reuben, who sported white long johns, longer and wider than Soggy's faded reds, said in his gravelly voice.

"Thank you."

Hawk raised his head.

Wearing an emerald-green robe, belted at the waist, Sage sank down beside him. Chestnut curls tumbled down her back. The moon peeking in from the window haloed soft skin, wide lips and clear gray eyes. To Hawk's fevered brain she looked like an angel. Every organ in his body sighed. What would it be like to see that face every day for the rest of his life? To wake to a face of an angel?

His whole body stuttered. The heat that flowed in his blood iced. What was he thinking? Granted marriage worked for some people, but he'd never consider himself part of that "some". He liked to know what was over the next horizon. He liked women who knew the score and there were no strings attached. Women you could pay in coin, not with a lifetime commitment.

"Just doing my job." His voice as stiff as his movements, he managed not to scoot away. Relief flooded him as Soggy came in, dressed in blue canvas pants, his nightshirt flapping around scrawny hips. Reuben came from down the hall dressed much the same in canvas pants and suspenders, but he'd taken time to throw on an old brown plaid shirt and buckle on his six-gun.

Hawk pushed to his feet. "Okay with you if I move back to the bunkhouse now that Santos is no longer an issue?" Wanting distance between him and Sage. No. Needing distance.

"You sure that's who he is? Was."

"Aren't you?"

"Yeah I am."

"So, okay if I head back to the bunkhouse?"

"Let me see to that arm." Before Hawk could protest Soggy pushed on his shoulder. Hawk subsided with a thump.

Soggy pulled out scissors and cut off the sleeve. The wound was long but shallow and had finally started to clot.

"Well?" Hawk asked Reuben through gritted teeth, as Soggy dressed the gash.

"Of course. Send someone to drag Billy to the bunkhouse where he can sleep it off and send someone to take his place.

"Sage, we got a shot at a couple of hours of sleep. What say we take it?" Reuben said.

"Is he going to be okay?" she looked at Soggy.

"Right as rain. It's barely a scratch."

"Sleep well, Hawk, and whether you want to hear it or not, thanks again for saving my life. And please don't say you were just doing your job."

Hawk tightened his jaw and gave a terse nod.

As they disappeared down the hallway, Hawk heard her say, "He's acting strangely."

"All young men his age act strangely," Reuben replied.

CHAPTER 26

It had been fifteen long days since Reuben had received the telegram from George Story. Seven since Hawk had ended Santos. Days filled with tension, worry and waiting.

He had half a mind to go to St. Louie himself and find out what was going on. It would involve being rattled around like a pebble in a jar in the stagecoach then crammed on a train that he'd have no control over but by gum he wanted answers.

He stood on his porch watching the sun in the west wind downward against a pinkish sky that before long would be a brilliant red, ringed with purple. A brisk breeze rustled the leaves in the old oak.

The planks groaned as behind him, Hawk rocked his chair, taking his turn on watch, a Winchester across his lap.

The smell of coffee, beans and cornbread drifted through the open door, and made Reuben's stomach growl, reminding him that with one thing and another he hadn't eaten since morning.

Boots clopped and the whiff of fresh coffee and vittles grew stronger. Carrying a plain wooden tray with dinner on it, Soggy stepped onto the porch.

"Got your dinner." He nodded in Hawk's direction. Hawk leaned the rifle against the side of the house, stood up and took the tray.

"Thanks, Soggy."

Soggy nodded before turning to Reuben. "Dinner's ready."

Reuben pointed at the tray. "You can bring that inside and eat with us. One of the boys in the bunkhouse can spell you."

"Thanks. I'm fine here."

As they headed toward the dining room, Soggy said, "He's fighting it."

"The boy's got it bad," Reuben agreed.

Silverware clinked against plain brown ceramic bowls as Sage set the table. A plate of hot cornbread and a block of butter already in place. She wore a tan split skirt, the boots he'd gotten her, and a pink blouse, and to his mind looked pretty as a picture.

She glanced over Reuben's shoulder.

"He's still insisting on eating on the porch?"

"Yup." Reuben walked to the small, black kitchen pump, washed his hands and threw some water on his face.

Soggy wrapped a plain brown potholder around his prized tin pot, carried it to the table, and began ladling beans into the bowls.

"Looks mighty good, Soggy," Reuben said.

"Why is he avoiding me?" Sage asked, as she sank down into her chair.

"Is he?" Reuben took a large mouthful of hot beans, swallowed quickly, got up and poured himself a glass of water and gulped it down.

"Might want to let them cool a minute," Soggy said mildly then winked at Sage.

She grinned then turned her attention back to Reuben and asked again, "Why is he avoiding me?"

Like a dog with a bone, Reuben thought in resignation. Before he could respond, Soggy said, "Because he's smitten."

"I beg your pardon." Sage blinked at the old man.

"You heard me," he said testily, adding, "And the fact scares him more than a chicken facing a determined fox."

"So, who's the chicken here and who's the fox?"

"It was just a mete-fore."

"Do you even know what that means?" Reuben demanded.

"Of course, I do," Soggy responded indignantly.

Sage interrupted. "Well, since he's the one that seems to be keeping his distance, I'd say he's the chicken and I'm the fox."

A laugh rumbled in Reuben's throat and Soggy grinned.

Before more could be said, the door slammed again and boots clipped across planks. They all looked up to see Hawk standing in front of them.

"You've got company," he said before stepping aside.

George Story and Senator Baylor stood in the doorway. The senator slapped at his shoulder dislodging road dust that floated in the air then settled on the floor. Both wore smiles a mile wide.

"It's over," the senator said.

CHAPTER 27

Everyone talked at once.

Sage jumped up and ran to Baylor and threw herself in his arms. "You're safe now."

"I'm safe? You're safe!" He hugged her and gave her a twirl that lifted her off her feet. Soggy was already on his.

"Sit. Sit." The cook grabbed bowls out of the cabinet. Silverware clinked as he plunked it out of the drawer.

"You don't need to tell me twice." The senator set his daughter on her feet and dropped into an empty chair.

Hawk took a comprehensive look around, his gaze lingering on Sage before he wheeled on his heel and headed for the door.

"Boy, there's no point in you eating out on the porch now. Grab your bowl and join us."

Hawk turned. "Thanks, maybe another time." Again, he started for the door.

"Hawk," Sage said.

Again, he turned. His expression wary.

"Join us. Please."

His shoulders slumped, his expression resigned,

before it fell back into his usual expressionless mask. "Alright."

Soggy looked at Reuben and winked. Reuben chewed a grin. He stuffed a piece of cornbread in his mouth when Sage glanced his way.

George and the senator fell on their food and ate hungrily. The others watched each spoonful they raised to their mouths. Anxious to hear the news.

Reuben shifted in his seat. Sage tapped her fingers against the table. Soggy twitched his shoulders. Hawk sat perfectly motionless, his eyes alert.

Baylor finally pushed his bowl away and patted his flat stomach. "That was mighty good, Soggy."

"Glad to hear it, now get on with it," the cook said in an irritated voice.

Baylor obliged. "George here," the senator reached over and slapped the reporter on the back, "took initiative and infiltrated the KKK. I've offered him a job on my staff, if he'll take it."

Reuben cut through the congratulations and asked in a rough voice, "Who was it?" Fire sparked behind his eyes. It was time for payback.

"I've taken care of it." Baylor met Reuben's gaze directly.

"Is he still breathing?"

Silence settled around the table. Tension built as thick as humid air before a storm.

"He's going to be stripped of power. To a man with his ego, that's worse than death."

"I'd like to strip him too. Out of a couple inches of hide."

"If I thought you'd stop there, I'd happily give you his name. But I know you, Reuben. Sage was threatened. You won't stop at a hiding."

"Oh, I think you'll tell me." Reuben pushed to his feet.

Sage's chair clattered behind her as she shot out of hers. "Don't you ever threaten my daddy."

The room stilled.

He took one look at the fire sparking in her eyes and knew he could lose her forever.

He took a deep breath, then another. Clenching and unclenching his fists, he fought the fury that rode him.

"Your daddy is safe from me," he said finally.

Air held in collective lungs whished out.

Reuben stomped to the cupboard and pulled out a bottle and a glass. He sloshed some of the amber brew into the glass, downed it in one gulp then strode back to his chair and thumped down.

He turned his ire on George. "What do you get out of all this?"

"Well, a healthy payment from you." He grinned.

"Then I want a name," Reuben ground out.

George turned serious.

"This man is powerful. Big in politics. Has his eye on a governorship. You shoot him and you'll hang for sure. The senator confronted him and let him know in no uncertain terms if anything happened to him or his daughter, the whole affair would be on the front page of every paper in the country. Trying to have a senator killed and being part of the KKK, that's news."

"And you think he won't kill you?" Reuben gave the senator a skeptical look.

"I made it perfectly clear, I'm not the only one who has the information. George here is my ace in the hole."

Reuben gave George a sour look then turned his attention back to the senator. "Being part of the KKK isn't exactly an unheard-of event in the South."

"True, but this particular senator," George let the title drop deliberately, "is originally from the north. A foot in both camps so to speak. What some would call a carpetbagger. His northern cronies wouldn't be impressed."

"I'm asking you again, what do you get out of this?"

"Oh, this isn't the only rotten pie the good senator has his finger in." George leaned back in his chair, his expression smug. "I did more research on his background. There's going to be several articles coming out. When I'm done there won't be a place the senator is welcome at except possibly the Badlands. He will have to resign and he sure as hell won't be governor."

Reuben gave George a nod of approval. The boy had kept his word to both him and the senator. He hadn't told him who it was, but he'd given him enough information to ferret it out himself.

The senator gave George a ferocious frown.

"Reuben." Sage's voice was quiet. Everyone stilled.

"Yes?"

"Please. Let it go. I couldn't bear it if anything

happened to you."

And just like that he melted. He had no more power against her than he'd had against her mother.

"Alright," he agreed reluctantly, tamping down the need for revenge coating his system.

"Promise me."

"I give you my word. Unless he comes after you again, I'll leave him to the tender mercies of your daddy and the reporter here. But know this." His mouth tightened along with the skin around his jaws. "If he does come for you again, nothing will keep me from tearing him apart and feeding the pieces to the buzzards."

"Fair enough." His eyes set in her beautiful face gazed back at him. "Shake on it."

He reached across the table, took her hand and gave it a firm shake. She gave it a little squeeze before she released it.

His heart lightened. He leaned back and caught Soggy grinning. "What?" he demanded.

Soggy mouthed, "Chicken." Then pointed at Sage. "Fox."

"Yeah."

CHAPTER 28

Hawk stood near the corral. A weak morning sun, that couldn't decide whether it wanted to shine or not, occasionally warming his shoulders.

Horses snorted. In the distance, he could hear the low of cattle. Jose nodded as he galloped by heading for the north pasture. Smells of horses, earth and the spicy scent of grass filled his nostrils and momentarily lessened the tension riding between his shoulders that the heat of the sun couldn't touch, nor could it reach the coldness inside him. His month was up and then some. It was time to move on. Grabbing the reins of his horse and squaring his shoulders, he strode toward the barn, where he'd seen Reuben disappear moments before.

Reuben stood in the stall saddling his Appaloosa. He looked up as Hawk strode in, leading his horse.

"Going somewhere?"

"My month's up."

"So it is. You know you're welcome to stay."

"Appreciate it, but I've got another job lined up."

Reuben nodded. He didn't seem too concerned, which irritated Hawk. He'd done a damn good job while he was here and thought he'd formed a bond of sorts with the formidable rancher.

"You running?"

Hawk jerked and his lips thinned. "From what?"

Reuben gave him a knowing look then went back to saddling his horse.

"I still owe you a few days' pay. Stop by the house on your way out and tell Soggy to pay you."

Hawk didn't respond. George Story and the senator had left but Sage had stayed. At the moment, she was in the house and he had no intention of going anywhere near it.

Done with the saddle, Reuben led his horse out of the stall. He held out his hand. "Good luck."

At that moment, Sage came trotting into the barn. "Reuben, I—" She ground to a halt. Her eyes narrowed. "What's going on?"

"Hawk here is moving on. His month is up." Leading his horse, he strode out of the barn.

Her eyes widened then sparked with anger.

He put his foot in the stirrup. Best to have some distance between them if they were going to have this conversation.

She grabbed his shoulder.

"Are you running away?"

Like father like daughter.

"My month is up." He eased his foot out and swung around to face her. The heavy sweet smell of hay vied with the verbena scent that always swirled around her, fresh and distracting. He looked pointedly at her hand. She withdrew it.

"Without saying goodbye."

He clamped his lips together.

"You're running," she accused.

"I've got another job. One that pays better." Or at least he would have. There was never a shortage of jobs in his profession.

"One that requires killing."

Again, he said nothing.

"What are you running from?"

Frustration, fear, regret, longing all roiled through his system. Barely aware of what he was doing, he yanked her to him and did what he'd been longing to do since the last time.

The kiss went on and on. The stamp and snort of horses faded, along with his surroundings. For the first time since he was a younker, he felt the warmth of homecoming, all the while his blood scalded through his system and he drew her closer, wanting, needing more.

For a moment, taken by surprise, her body went limp, her lips parted, giving no resistance and then the need coursing through him transferred into her and she returned kiss for kiss, her fingers woven into his hair, pushing closer against him, demanding more.

The passion jerked him back to reality and scared him even more than he had been before. He pushed her away, leaped into the saddle and galloped off, not looking back.

CHAPTER 29

Texas was ripe with summer. Long muggy days and nights filled with enough blazing stars in the sky to take a man's breath away.

This evening, a cooling breeze blew as Reuben leaned on the porch rail, looking over the land he loved, that he was as rooted to as the gnarled ancient oak that grew near the west side of the house.

In the corral, Darling waited patiently for Sage and a carrot. Her head hanging over the top rail of the enclosure. Gawky and growing, Thunder galloped around the corral, snorting and tossing his back heels in the air like a small tornado. A miniature of his daddy.

Levi stepped out of the bunkhouse, rolled a smoke and lit it, his heel and shoulders resting against the sturdy building. He saw Reuben and raised a hand. Reuben nodded in acknowledgement.

An early evening star gleamed bright against a red horizon.

Soggy opened the door. "Dinner's ready." The smell of yeasty bread and pot roast followed him out.

"Smells mighty good, Soggy. I'll wash up and be right in." He pointed at the star. "My mammy always said that an early evening star was the portent of good news that the heavens couldn't wait to impart."

"Well, let's hope your mammy was right. We could use some good news."

The door banged as Soggy strode back in.

"Yeah," he said to no one in particular. Sage had been off her oats for weeks. He had half a notion to hop on his horse, ride out, find Hawk and kick his hind end for upsetting his girl. Instead, he primed the pump, stuck his head under it as cold water poured out then washed his hands and strode inside.

"Evening, missy." He thumped down in his chair.

He rubbed his hands together then grabbed a couple of rolls and passed them to Sage, who took one and passed them to Soggy.

"Soggy, pass that corn." He glanced over at Sage who stared at her plate but made no attempt to eat. His fork clattered against the plate as he sat it down. "He'll be back."

Young love. It was both glorious and brutal. That was one of the few good things of aging. It deadened those nerve endings that were alive with pain. Course it also deadened the amazing passion, pleasure and joy. Guess it was a tradeoff at best.

"It's been two months. He's not coming back."

"Young men are a real strange breed. Their head ain't usually what they do their thinking with."

Sage colored up.

Of course, Reuben noticed. His eyes narrowed.

"I don't need to track him down and beat him within an inch of his life, do I?"

"For a kiss? After which, he jumped on his horse and rode out like his pants were on fire." An aggrieved expression crossed her features and she shoved a small potato into her mouth and chewed with ferocity. "That was two months ago," she repeated.

"Marryin's a scary business. A man has to be sure he's serious about it."

"Who said anything about marrying?"

Reuben who had just brought a large piece of beef to his mouth, set it back down.

"Well, girl, if we ain't talkin' about marriage, what are we talking about?" He gave her a fierce frown.

"Nothing. We aren't talking about anything."

"Nothing and anything ain't what we called it in my day."

Before she could respond the outer door slammed and boot heels clicked, growing louder as they came closer.

Sage clutched the end of the table. Her nails digging into the soft pine.

Hawk stood in the doorway, clutching his hat. His face white, his expression determined. He nodded to Soggy, looked for a long moment at Sage then turned his attention to Reuben.

"May I speak to you, sir?"

Reuben picked up his fork, chewed his beef and swallowed. Not that he wasn't glad to see the young man, mind. But considering he'd upset Sage, he saw no reason to jump up and slap the young hombre on his back and walk away from damn fine vittles.

"Anything you've got to say to me, you can say

here and now," he said, determined to finish his meal while it was still hot.

Soggy kicked him under the table.

"Oww. What was that for?"

Soggy notched his head in the direction of the study.

"Oh." He pushed back his chair and with a longing look at his heaped plate, strode out of the room. He wheeled on his heel. "You coming?"

Hawk fell in behind him.

Once in the study, he shut the door and poured a couple of dollops of whiskey into two shot glasses and handed one to Hawk. Hawk tossed it down then seemed to steady.

He cleared his throat. "I'd like your permission to marry Sage."

"Oh, would you now?"

"Yes," he looked Reuben straight in the eye.

"How do you plan to support her?"

"You gave her the old homestead right?"

"I did."

"I thought I'd build us a cabin on it and raise horses. She's got a way with them."

"Where ya going to get the money. With your gun?" He rocked on his heels and pointed at the six-gun on Hawk's hip.

"No, I'm giving that up. I've got some money tucked back for a rainy day. Not a lot but enough to get us started." He ran his finger around the inside of his collarless shirt. "Appears its pouring."

"Well, for what it's worth, you've got my blessing,

but I'm not the man who raised her and that's the blessing you'll need."

"Already got it."

Reuben was seldom surprised but he was surprised now.

"Do tell."

"He said I wasn't his first choice for his daughter, and I can certainly understand that, but you seemed to think that I had some value and if Sage wanted me, he wouldn't stand in our way."

"Well then let's go find out if Sage wants you or not. And as far as that cabin. If she accepts, I'll build you a ranch house where the old one stands as a wedding present."

"I don't want any handouts." Hawk stood stiffly, crushing the rim of his hat, looking so much like a contrary mule it made Reuben's lips twitch.

"A wedding gift," he replied firmly.

"I thankee. If she'll have me," he added, looking a bit green around the gills.

"You got a last name?"

"As I said before, I go by Hawk." Hawk notched up his chin, his expression closed.

Reuben snorted.

"When you take your vows, you'll go by Hayes."

Hawk blinked and his jaw dropped. Finally, he stuttered, "I don't know what to say."

"No need to say anything. Now let's go see if she'll have you."

~*~

The spit dried in Hawk's mouth and his knees locked making walking nigh impossible.

"Are you coming or not? If you could move quicker than an old man leaning on a cane, I might get back to my dinner before it's stone cold." Reuben stood in the doorway and motioned him through it.

Putting one foot in front of the other, he forced his legs forward.

Reuben slid into his chair and scooped up potatoes.

Soggy picked up his coffee then sat it back down, waiting expectantly.

Hawk stopped in front of Sage's chair. Though color rode her cheeks, she stared at him coolly.

He cleared his throat. "Could I speak to you?"

"Go ahead."

"In private."

"As Reuben said, anything you have to say to me you can say here."

He bit back a sigh. Sage had never been easy. Nor had he given her any reason to in this particular situation. Surprisingly, it was Reuben who came to his rescue.

"I guess I'm destined for a cold meal. Grab your coffee, Soggy, and we'll finish it on the porch."

"Yuh sure? I've never witnessed a proposal before." His face reflected disappointment, though his eyes twinkled.

Now that he had the boss's blessing, the old coot had decided to give him a bad time, Hawk thought in exasperation. Well, he guessed he couldn't blame him either. They all loved Sage and took her welfare seriously.

"Yeah, I'm sure."

Both men grabbed their coffee and trooped out.

Hawk waited for the door to slam shut, but it didn't. He gave another internal sigh. So be it.

He got down on his knees and reached for Sage's hand.

She drew it back and glared at him. "You left me. Like an unwanted dog. You ran," she accused.

He pushed to his feet.

"I did leave you. I did run. But you were never unwanted. You were wanted too much and that scared the bejeezus right out of me." He threw up his hands, not sure he could explain. "I've been on my own since I was a younker. The thought of being dependent on someone else—I didn't know how to deal with it. If something happened to you, my blood would stop flowing and my heart stop beating. How does one deal with those feelings?" He ran his fingers through his hair, searching for words.

"I thought if I could get away from you, I could regain my sense of self. Be able to function on my own again. But I couldn't. I can't. The further I got from you, the worse it got. I haven't slept a full night since I left nor eaten a regular meal. The sad truth is I'm nothing without you. I depend on you more than the air I breathe. If you could bring yourself to love me even half as much as I love you, I'd be happy.

"Will you marry me, Sage?"

Somehow his hand had found hers. Or maybe hers had found his.

"Yes, oh yes." She jumped up and threw herself in his arms.

Before he could kiss her as he longed to, Soggy and Reuben came clumping back in.

"Well, I'm glad that's settled maybe now I can finish my supper."

EPILOGUE

Reuben paced the study going over a mental check list, more nervous than he'd been when he fought his first Indian. He'd had Katherine's table re-stained and Soggy had managed to clean the old tapestry. Jose and Abe had been working on the new cabin he was building for Sage as a wedding present. It wasn't done, but it was close as dammit. By the time the newlyweds got back from the honeymoon it would be.

Soggy had enough food to feed an army. The minister had arrived. The senator had got in last night. The hands were dressed in their best bib and tuckers. He looked down at his black suit and uncomfortable starched shirt. And so was he. The letter crinkled in his pocket.

His boots, spit polished till they shone, clicked against the wooden planks as he made his way to the whiskey decanter.

He poured himself a whiskey and dropped into his chair behind the old scarred desk. It was time.

He downed the whiskey in one gulp, the golden brew warming his innards and settling his shaking hands. Straightening his shoulders, he took out the letter and stared at it for a long time.

Finally, he picked up the plain metal letter opener and carefully slit the envelope. The paper rustled as he pulled it out then smoothed the wrinkled parchment. The first thing that hit him was the scent. Lavender. His heart gave a hitch. She'd always worn it.

He ran a hand over his face then pulled spectacles out of his pocket and began to read.

Dear Reuben,

If you are reading this letter then I have passed on. Don't be sad. I've had a good life.

There's something I have to tell you. I should have told you years ago but I didn't know how. You made it clear that if I left, we were through. You didn't want me back. In the beginning, I kept thinking you'd change your mind and come after me. That if you loved me enough you would. That I was worth more to you than a ranch out in the middle of nowhere. But you never came and I couldn't wait any longer.

He put down the letter and rubbed at the growing pressure between his eyes. He had, in fact, gone after her. He'd swallowed his pride and gone to beg her to come home with him, but as he stood in the shadows, of the address he'd been given for her, he saw her and Baylor on the porch, moths dancing round the yellow light that shown down on their embrace. He'd turned on his heels and didn't look back nor ever went to St. Louie again.

We have a daughter, Reuben. She's so much like you it makes my heart ache. Oh, she looks like me, except for those stormy gray eyes. But she's you through and through. She's all stubbornness and high courage. She has your kindness too, that you keep hidden underneath that tough exterior.

I married James Baylor. He's a good man and we were happy together. I loved him. Oh, not like I loved you. Not that all-consuming fire that you and I had whose sparks reached high into the night sky and torched everything around it. Lightning doesn't strike twice and I'm not sure I'd have the strength to live through those feelings again. What James and I had was more comfortable, like sitting in front of a pot-bellied stove on a cold winter's night. Doesn't sound very romantic, does it? But we were content and that was enough. I hope you've found someone to be content with. Or even found lightning in a bottle again, though I admit I'd be a little jealous. But whether you are alone or have married, find your daughter, get to know her before it's too late. Her name's Sage and she was the best gift you could have ever given me. I never stopped loving you, Reuben, and hope with all my heart you are happy.

Yours forever,

K.

Carefully, he set the letter down, took off his spectacles and rubbed his eyes. Pride. They'd both had it by the barrels and it had cost them their shot at happiness.

He ached for both himself and Katherine and what they'd lost. But now, at last, he could move on. With the letter, she'd given him peace. The anger and hurt finally gone. Most of all, she'd given him Sage.

A knock sounded at the door.

He laid the letter on a scarred round table by the

chair and croaked, "Come in." He cleared his throat and tried again. "Come in."

Baylor stuck his head in.

He motioned the senator inside, got up and filled another shot glass and handed it to him before pouring another dollop in his own. He clinked it against Baylor's glass. "To Katherine and Sage."

"To Katherine and Sage," James echoed.

The whiskey burned as he tossed it down.

The senator downed his then said, "It's time. Let's walk our daughter down the aisle."

He nodded and the two men strode to her room. Reuben knocked on the door and called, "Time's a wastin'."

Silk rustled as she stepped out. Her eyes sparkling, her lips curved, she clutched wildflowers of every imaginable color that Billy had picked for her that morning. Her cream-colored gown trailed the curves of her body. She looked so much like her mother his heart hurt.

"You're beautiful," the senator said, his voice husky.

She smiled then looked at Reuben, her eyebrows quirked.

"Your daddy's got the right of it." He held out an arm. She took it with one hand and placed her other in the senator's. They walked down the hallway, through the entryway and to the rock river fireplace where the minister, middle-aged and wearing black, waited. Hawk beside him.

They stopped in front of the minister. She dropped

their arms and reached up and kissed the senator. "Daddy."

"Be happy, darling," he said, his eyes suspiciously bright.

Then she reached over and to Reuben's surprise and pleasure said, "Pa," and kissed his cheek.

His heart dropped to his toes and, once again, he had to clear his throat a couple of times. Instead of wishing her happy, he wheeled on Hawk, a fierce frown on his countenance. "You hurt her in any way and I'll cut out your gizzard and fry it up for breakfast. You got that?"

"Yes, sir." Hawk's Adam's apple bobbed and the ranch hands guffawed.

Reuben and the senator stepped back. Hawk took their place and held out his hands. Sage took them. Their locked gazes promised more than words ever could. The joy palatable.

A breeze blew through the open window, caressing his cheek and carrying the illusive scent of lavender. He smiled and gazed out the aperture. It was a day of new beginnings. For Sage and Hawk, and for him as well. Who knew, maybe lightning did strike twice. Even for an ole codger like him. But whether it did or not, he had a heartful of happiness right here and now.

He took one last inhale of the fading fragrance then turned his attention to his daughter and son-to-be.

The minister cleared his throat and the ceremony began.

The End

AUTHOR NOTE

Just a handful of factoids, for those of you who might be wondering:

Anti-lynching laws were introduced to congress in 1882. I'd like to think members of congress were writing them and trying to get them passed in 1880.

Horace Jackson, Justice Death, is a fictional character. Isaac Parker was a real person, known as the Hanging Judge. He presided over thousands of cases and sentenced one hundred and sixty people to death.

Samuel Maxey was indeed a Texas senator and served from 1875-1887.

Petroleum jelly was patented in 1872 and was referred to as rod wax.

A Texas Toothpick was a folding knife crafted by Roy Jones in the mid-1800s.

The KKK was formed in 1865.

The Liberty Head gold eagle was the equivalent of ten dollars and minted from 1838 to 1907

Vittles or victuals refers to food.

Hosses to horses.

Breadbasket to the stomach.

Shampoo was sold in drug stores in the 1880s, but was different from the commercial shampoo of today. It was made from oils, herbs or soap flakes and was often powdered or soap based.

Thankee refers to thank you. And I thankee for reading Reuben's story.

Sandra

ABOUT SANDRA

Sandra, who writes as both S. Cox and Sandra Cox, is an animal lover and avid gardener. She spent a number of years in the Midwest chasing down good Southern BBQ. By the time she moved to North Carolina where Southern BBQ is practically a staple, she'd become a vegetarian.

She and her husband are ruled by four cats and a dog. An award-winning author, her stories consist of all things Western and more.

Sandra can be found at

http://www.sandracoxwriter.com

OR http://www.cowboytrivia.blogspot.com

OR https://sandracox.blogspot.com

OR https://www.pinterest.com/scoxauthor/

If you'd like notification of new releases you can sign up on the contact form/newsletter signup at *sandracoxwriter* or *sandracoxblogspot* (addies above) and type in the word NEWSLETTER. Her twitter handle is: Sandra_Cox. Blue Sky is scoxauthor. And her Amazon page: https://www.amazon.com/stores/Sandra-Cox/author/B002BM3AKC

Last but not least, if you enjoyed this story enough to leave a good review, thank you so much. Great reviews are an author's bread, butter and favorite ice cream, all rolled up in one.